DEMONIC TALES FROM DIFFERENT LANDS

Winifred Finlay

MAMMOTH

For Evan

First published in Great Britain 1983
by Methuen Children's Books Ltd
Magnet paperback edition published 1986
This new edition published 1993 by Mammoth
an imprint of Reed Consumer Books Ltd
Michelin House, 81 Fulham Road, London SW3 6RB
and Auckland, Melbourne, Singapore and Toronto

Copyright © 1983 Winifred Finlay

ISBN 0 7497 1491 3

A CIP catalogue record for this title
is available from the British Library

Printed in Great Britain
by Cox & Wyman Ltd, Reading, Berkshire

Contents

1 The Houndpriest of Melrose

On the banks of the River Tweed well over eight hundred years ago, where now only sad ruins remain, there stood the once splendid abbey of Melrose. The monks, humble and God-fearing, prayed long and fasted often: they helped those who were old and sick, offered shelter and food to travellers rich and poor alike and devoted their lives to the care of the souls of all people.

But while they dressed in their simple, coarsely-woven habits and, barefooted, chanted their services in the great stone abbey, there were some who mocked at such piety and selflessness, declaring that life on earth was all that mattered and as it was short, it ought to be enjoyed to the full.

Such a one was the wealthy Lady who lived in the castle above the abbey. She kept a fine stable of horses and a large pack of hounds and hunted regularly by day, while by night the great hall rang with loud laughter and singing as she and her friends feasted and caroused.

Because she gave generously to the abbey and because, on the rare occasions she attended mass there, she appeared to be contrite and devout, the Abbot of Melrose had not the courage to reprove her, trusting that the old priest who was her chaplain was exercising a certain restraint on her and her guests.

Then the old priest died and both Abbot and monks were extremely concerned when the Lady offered his position to a young man whose life was such that, had this offer not been made, he would have been asked to leave the Church where he had so blatantly neglected his duties.

He was strikingly handsome, dark-haired, red-cheeked and red-lipped. When he smiled – and he smiled a great deal – he revealed big strong white teeth, and when he laughed – and he laughed even more than he smiled – he drew back his thick red lips and the canine teeth were seen to be long and sharp and pointed.

His great delight lay in hunting. But not content with the Lady's horses and hounds, he soon acquired a stable of his own and a pack of huge grey wolfhounds. These great beasts accompanied him everywhere, so that those who lived nearby and saw him riding past with his wild howling pack called him the Houndpriest, and cringed at the fearful sound of that deep-throated baying.

Well did they know that when he returned to the Lady's castle he would feed on the richest food and drink himself insensible on the finest wines, but more bitter still was the knowledge that while they went hungry and their children died of cold and starvation, the Houndpriest fed his pack on the choicest cuts of meat and ordered the servants away from the fire so that his beasts could spend the night in front of it, sprawled out in comfort.

As the months passed, fear and dislike of the Houndpriest grew among those who lived in the

Border villages, in the lonely farms and cottages of the Lowland hills.

'It was an evil day for us when the Lady invited the Houndpriest to be her chaplain,' they whispered. 'Those hounds know only one master and he lies in a drunken stupor each night. The time will come when one of the beasts will tire of sleeping in front of the fire and will leave the castle – and then who can tell what might befall?' And they exchanged uneasy glances and waited for they knew not what might be their fate.

It was on the morning after All Hallows' Eve, when the priest had been at the castle for exactly one year, that the first sheep was found on the lower slopes of the Eildon Hills, its throat torn and so savagely mauled that there was scarcely any blood left in its body.

Four weeks later another sheep was savaged.

And then another.

'Always at the time of the full moon,' the people whispered, and they waited fearfully. And then what they had most dreaded, happened.

It was a clear moonlit night. A pilgrim was on his way to Melrose Abbey when, less than half a mile from it, he was attacked.

The next morning charcoal-burners found his body, throat torn and drained of blood, and remembered the terrible baying of the hounds during the night.

'Our lives are at stake now,' they cried, and farmers and peasants and shepherds banded together and carried the body of the pilgrim to the abbey and showed it to the Abbot.

'Neither sheep nor man is safe from the Houndpriest's beasts once darkness falls,' they declared. 'We beseech you, good Lord Abbot, to protect us. Such fearsome hounds must be shut up in kennels as other dogs are.'

Horrified the Abbot, a good and holy man, promised to do what he could and sent at once for the Houndpriest, who listened scornfully and then laughed, revealing his strong white teeth.

'My hounds kill mangy sheep and a half-witted pilgrim? Nonsense! Dogs kill only when they are hungry and mine are never that. This is surely the work of the wolves that roam the Eildon Hills and the Lammermuirs. Tell the shepherds to keep better watch or to pen their sheep. Meanwhile I and my hounds will help them by hunting every day and killing all the wolves we encounter.'

As he spoke he placed a leather bag on the table, and red were his lips and sharp and pointed his canine teeth as he laughed. 'My Lady bade me bring you this money. The welfare of the abbey is dear to her as you well know, and you would be wise to remember this before you speak against her household again, for there are other abbeys which would be grateful to have such a generous patron.'

A whole year went by without incident and then, just when people felt there was no need to fear the nights of the full moon, another sheep was found savaged and drained of blood.

Four weeks after that a journeyman working late at night failed to return hom and his body was found at first light, in the same condition as that of the pilgrim of the year before.

Again the people banded together and carried the body to the Abbot and showed it to him.

'There are no wolves near Melrose, good Lord Abbot,' they said. 'This butchery is the work of the Houndpriest's beasts. If he will not listen to you, you must talk to the Lady who employs him. Tell her to order him to shut up his hounds. Now none of us dare venture abroad at night and we fear what will happen again when the moon is full.'

Shocked and saddened, the Abbot promised to do what he could and he rode off at once to visit the Lady in her castle.

'It reflects on the Church, on this Abbey, and on me, your spiritual father, that you employ this priest whose entire life is devoted to sport and pleasure. Surely you must be aware that his hounds are loose at night, killing sheep – aye, and men too. I am come to beg you to prevail on him to mend his ways, and if he will not, to dismiss him from your service.'

'Dismiss my priest, Father? Why should I, when he carries out his duties to my satisfaction? As for his hounds, I am convinced they cause no trouble. It is the wolves that roam the hills that do the killing of which you speak.'

Whereupon she offered the Abbot food and drink – which he refused. But when she gave him money for the abbey, that he had to accept though his heart was heavy.

Afraid and apprenhensive, the people waited, and although the weeks passed and the months and nothing happened, there was much talk in the market places and at fairs and inns. Each time the Hound-priest rode past followed by his baying hounds, men and women crossed themselves, and when he laughed

5

at them for their fear, they thought how strangely young he looked, his cheeks and lips even redder than before, his teeth yet whiter and stronger . . . and longer.

It was on the first full moon after Hallowe'en that another sheep was savaged, and four weeks later a shepherd met his death in the same terrible fashion as the journeyman and the pilgrim.

'Now three men have met a cruel and savage death,' the people cried, as they gathered outside the abbey. 'If the Abbot and his monks and the Lady cannot protect us from the Houndpriest and his beasts, then we must protect ourselves.' But even as they were discussing the ways and means of doing this they saw one of the Lady's menservants, mounted on a sweating roan, galloping towards them.

'Make way, good people,' he cried. 'My business is with the Abbot. My Lady is in great distress. An hour back her priest was thrown from his horse and now lies dead, his neck broken and twisted awry.'

There was a general sigh of relief.

'In that case, there is nothing the Abbot can do,' one man said.

'Except bury the Houndpriest deep where he can cause no more trouble,' another added.

'My Lady wishes him to be buried in the churchyard here,' the servant said.

'The abbey churchyard is the last place where the Houndpriest should be buried,' cried the brother of the dead shepherd.

As usual, the Lady gave much gold and had her way. The Houndpriest was buried in the churchyard of Melrose Abbey, but there were only monks at the funeral service and none of them mourned the death of a priest who had put the pleasures of the world before his duties as a churchman.

That evening the hounds devoured their rich meal greedily and then one after another collapsed, howling and twitching, and all were dead within a few minutes.

'They have gone to join their master,' one of the servants said, but the word 'poison' was on other lips for none had liked the Houndpriest.

When the monks at the abbey heard what had happened to the hounds they looked at one another in dismay.

'I do not like it,' the youngest said. He had been a cowherd before he took his vows and so looked after the abbey's cattle: only too well did he know what was being said openly in the market place. 'Because the Abbot himself is good and kind and gentle, he does not know what evil there is in others. It may be that people are right when they say the Houndpriest should not have been buried in the abbey churchyard.'

'I know not what you may mean,' the oldest monk said, and he shuffled away to his cold bare cell and prayed for forgiveness for the lie he had told because he was afraid of the truth.

'Now our sheep can safely graze on the Eildon Hills and the Lammermuirs,' one farmer said the next day.

'And men can walk safely by night once more,' another added. But all the others remained silent, knowing they could only wait. And pray.

One month later, at midnight, with the moon full and round in the sky, the Sacristan of Melrose woke in his cell to find a terrible apparition bending over him – a

7

tall form dressed in a white shroud, with a pale face and staring eyes and thick red lips drawn back to reveal strong white teeth on which there was fresh red blood, and putting a trembling hand to his neck, the Sacristan knew the blood was his own.

Seizing his crucifix he held this up before the menacing figure and as it shrank away and disappeared into the darkness he hurried to toll the great bell of the abbey to summon his brothers and warn them of the danger in which they stood.

When the Abbot heard what the Sacristan had to say and examined the marks on his throat, he gave orders that day and night prayers were to be said and psalms sung to protect the abbey and all within it, while at the same time he sent for advice from men of wisdom and learning in other abbeys.

When the apparition found all ways into the Abbey barred to it, it climbed up to the castle and roamed along the passages and corridors shrieking and screaming as it sought a victim unprotected by a crucifix.

At last in the corner of the scullery it spied a little kitchenmaid and had just reached out grasping hands to seize her when the first cock crowed. Loudly it shrieked . . . once . . . twice . . . three times and then it disappeared, and throughout the castle there was an unearthly quiet.

'This is no place for us,' the servants cried, and seizing what possessions they could they fled to the safety of their homes or the farms and cottages of friends, paying no attention to the entreaties of the Lady that someone should stay and protect her. Only the little kitchenmaid remained. She was too frightened to move and besides, as she was an orphan, she had nowhere to go.

So the Lady saddled her horse and set the kitchen-maid on it, mounted behind her and rode down to the abbey. There she flung herself on the floor and begged the Abbot to protect her.

'Pray for me, Lord Abbot,' she pleaded, weeping with remorse and fearing it was too late to mend her ways, 'and find some way of putting an end to the power of the Houndpriest whose wickedness I did not know till now.'

'The Houndpriest?' the Abbot said in amazement. 'But he is dead a month since and now lies at peace in our churchyard.'

At this the Lady wept even more bitterly, so that the Abbot promised to do all he could and sent her and the kitchenmaid to the abbey guesthouse, with two monks to keep watch and pray for them. And then he called together all his monks, for he knew now he had not time to wait for advice from men of wisdom and learning in other abbeys.

'I have dwelt so long away from the world that I do not understand how this evil thing is come to us at Melrose Abbey,' he confessed, 'and so now I beg any of you who are younger and know what people say, to tell me the truth and advise me what I should do.'

All the monks looked at the youngest brother and somehow he found the courage to speak.

'I am convinced the Houndpriest is a vampire,' he said. 'It was he and not his dogs or the wolves who killed sheep and men and drank their blood over the past years. He has sold his soul to the Devil for everlasting youth, and now that his body is dead, he must sleep by day and feed on warm red blood by night.'

'I cannot believe such a thing of one of our churchmen,' the Abbot cried in horror.

'Alas! It is only too true,' the Sacristan said, pointing to the teeth marks on his own neck. 'Had I not wakened when I did there would have been no Sacristan standing here now.'

'We must act before he claims another victim,' the youngest monk said. 'With your permission and your blessing, Father, I shall keep watch over his grave tonight.'

'One man alone might not prevail against such an evil creature,' the Abbot answered, and it was decided that not only the youngest monk but also the Sacristan and two lay brothers, both armed with picks and axes, should stand guard over the grave of the Houndpriest, while the others prayed in the abbey.

Cold was the wind that swept down from the hills as the four men kept their vigil in the desolate churchyard, chill the mists that drifted up from the river and swirled around them. Mournfully the abbey bell tolled the passing of each long hour until at last it was midnight and they stood there tense, waiting as the twelfth stroke died away. They stared down at the grave and then gazed furtively around, listening to the sough of the wind and the muffled chanting and praying of the holy men in the abbey.

An hour passed.

And another.

'The Houndpriest vampire must intend to wait until the moon is full again,' the Sacristan said, and blew on his chilled hands. 'I think it would be safe for us to go now and warm ourselves by the kitchen fire for a few minutes, for I must confess I am not so young and hardy as once I was.'

'Do you three go,' the youngest monk answered. 'I shall stay here.'

'If you must stay, then take my axe,' one of the lay brothers urged.

'An axe? I have no need for that while I have my crucifix.'

'Nevertheless take it. There are times when cold steel is the only safeguard against Evil.'

And so the youngest monk took the axe and withdrew to the shadows as the other three departed for the warmth and comfort of the kitchen.

Although he was used to rising and praying at night and could go long hours without sleep, now he was alone he found himself yawning again and again, and in spite of his efforts to keep awake gradually his eyes closed, opened and began to close again.

This is the work of some evil power, he thought, and he struck his bare hand fiercely against the stone wall so that the pain should force him to stay awake. And then came the noise – though whether it was just in his head or was all around him in the churchyard he could not tell – a low, moaning, pulsating sound that rose steadily higher and higher, beating on his ear-drums until it seemed as though his head would burst open, and then, just when he could bear the shrill, high-pitched whine no longer, a tall figure in a white shroud burst from the grave and set off across the churchyard towards the nearest village.

In the silence that followed the youngest monk heard the soft lapping of the River Tweed and that old familiar sound broke his fear and the lethargy that was threatening to immobilise him, and he sprang forward, crucifix in hand, shuddering as he faced the Houndpriest vampire in its graveclothes, its face now pale, its lips drawn back in a grimace to reveal long, white ugly teeth.

'Stay, Houndpriest, stay! Proceed no farther, I command you,' he cried. 'There is no place for such creatures as you in the churchyard of the House of God.' But laughing scornfully, the vampire advanced on him, intent on knocking the crucifix out of his hand, and now the youngest monk knew the lay brother had been right and that he needed cold steel too, and he swung the axe as he had done when he had been a farm labourer. The steel head buried itself deep in the vampire's body and the next moment the white shroud was stained with blood.

With a dreadful cry the creature turned and stumbled back to its grave to disappear as quickly as it had appeared, and as the earth closed over it, from the abbey came the sound of monks at prayer.

When the Sacristan and the two lay brothers hurried out and heard what had happened, they blamed themselves bitterly for leaving the youngest monk alone to deal with such evil.

'I was in no danger,' he assured them. 'The crucifix was my protection, the axe with its cold steel my weapon. But the battle is only half won.' And he told them of the old tales recounted by the fireside when he was a boy and the hushed snippets of conversation heard in market places and at fairs. 'The rest must be seen to the moment the sun rises. One thing is certain. We must watch the grave until then lest the Evil One, his Master, tries to set him free to prey on men and beasts again.'

Silently they waited in the cold and the dark, each

man clasping his crucifix and praying for courage and for help to put an end to the Houndpriest vampire lying in the chill earth at their feet.

As soon as the first rays of the morning sun touched the hilltops they set to work with pickaxes and spades and it seemed to them that the soil could not possibly have been disturbed since the day of the burial. When at last they reached the coffin and levered up the lid, there lay the Houndpriest, looking even younger than when he had first taken up his appointment with the Lady in the castle high above Melrose.

Red were his cheeks and red the lips now closed so firmly over those fearful white teeth, but what was the look in his eyes no man knew, for they were sealed by his eyelids. Yet it was not the vampire's face that caused the four men to shrink back in horror and to call out to the Abbot and the monks who were now hastening, still singing, from the great abbey to the open grave – it was the sight of the handle of the axe which protruded from the Houndpriest's heart and the red, red blood that still dripped down slowly, slowly, to stain the white shroud.

'You are right,' the lay brother said. 'The battle is not yet won.' For he too remembered the old tales of his childhood.

'Do what must be done,' the Abbot said, and bowed his head in prayer.

Whereupon the lay brothers lifted up the body of the Houndpriest and carried it out of the churchyard to the crossroads and laid it there while the monks gathered a great pile of oak branches, and when they turned to place the vampire on it and the sun's rays touched the creature, everyone shuddered to see that terrible face collapse and wither and grow old, the hair turn scant and white and the now withered lips fall back to reveal only a few blackened teeth.

Summoning up all his courage, the good Abbot himself set a light to the great pile of oak branches and the flames sprang up and enclosed the remains of the vampire and purified them, burning fiercely until all that remained was a steel axe head and a heap of soft white ash, and this ash a clean wind from the north-west caught and scattered no man knew where. So at last the great abbey of Melrose and all the brave Borderland with its rivers and hills and forests were freed forever from the horror of the Houndpriest vampire.

2   The Beast of Auvergne

Three times Pierre, the footman, knocked on the heavy oak-panelled door, and when there was no answer he turned apologetically to the gentleman who was studying an Italian painting on the wall of the hall.

'I am afraid Monsieur de Sauveterre does not care to be disturbed when occupied with his accounts,' he said with deference. 'What do you wish me to do now, monsieur?'

'Do, you idiot? Why, open the door of course. And announce me at once.'

Pierre swallowed, knocked a fourth time and nervously opened the door.

'Monsieur Lar – ' he began, and ducked to avoid the heavy glass goblet which passed over his head, hit the tapestry on the opposite wall and splintered on the marble tiles of the floor.

'My dear Charles!' Antoine Laroche pushed the cowering servant out of the way and strode into the room, resplendent in his new padded breeches, leather jerkin and plumed hat. 'Is that how you welcome your oldest and dearest friend? I would have you know I am the hunter and not the quarry.'

'Antoine!' Charles de Sauveterre sprang from his desk and hurried across the room to embrace his

friend. 'I had no idea it was you. Pierre, you fool – '
But Pierre had alrady made himself scarce, and with
an exasperated shrug at the stupidity of servants,
Charles turned back to Antoine. 'So – what brings
you back to the Auvergne? I thought you were to
enjoy life in Paris for another month at least.'

'What brings me back is this.' Antoine slapped his
hand on the empty game-bag he carried and flou-
rished his gun. 'Without sport I cannot exist.'

'I heard there was enough sport for a rich young
bachelor such as you at the court of King Henri – at
least I found that to be the case before I was shackled
by the bonds of matrimony.'

Antoine threw back his head and laughed.

'I have not noticed that those shackles have inhib-
ited your pursuit of other fair ladies, Charles.

'But as for me, I have had my share of stalking the
Court beauties, and prefer nobler game to test a man's
skill and endurance. And so I returned home last
night and am come here to ask you to join me in a
day's sport.'

'Antoine, *mon ami*, if only I could. But see for
yourself – ' Wearily Charles indicated the account
books and documents on his desk. 'The notary comes
to see me within the hour, for I am faced by a most
devastating crisis.'

'Yet again?' Antoine asked with a broad smile.

'Yet again. What times we live in! I have a host of
servants in my château and yet it falls to pieces
around me: an army of gardeners cannot keep the
grounds as I wish, and though I own lands, farms and
forests, I swear I do not have a sou to my name.'

'That is the cry of everyone of consequence in
Paris,' Antoine said easily. 'Except that they have a

16

further cause for discontent. Their wives demand the most extravagant clothes and jewellery and – '

'It is not only in Paris that wives make such demands,' Charles interrupted. 'It is but a few weeks ago that Madame my wife wheedled the most expensive of rings out of me because it was her birthday, knowing full well that I had not the means to pay for it – nor am ever likely to have.'

'She is well, Madame your wife? I trust I may pay my respects to her before I leave?'

Charles frowned.

'My wife is away today – as she has been on many others. It would appear she finds more pleasure in the company of our new neighbour, the Widow Bellenot.'

'That creature? I most heartily dislike that woman. She is too aggressive and has too much book learning for one of her sex. They say her mother was burned as a witch, but that may be idle talk.' He broke off at the timid knock on the door and watched as a pretty maidservant came in quietly, carrying a tray on which were glasses, brandy and biscuits. Eyes lowered, she curtseyed to the two men and withdrew as quietly as she had entered.

'An attractive wench,' Antoine said approvingly. 'Where did you find her?'

'I believe she came from some nearby village,' Charles answered with studied carelessness. 'I forget which.'

So he is up to his old tricks again, Antoine thought, and as he drank his brandy he wondered if his friend's marriage had foundered already. Shortly afterwards he set off through the estate to hunt in the woods beyond.

*

17

Four hundred years ago, that part of Auvergne was remote and wild, cut off from the rest of the country by steep mountains, clothed with dense forests, and by fast-flowing rivers in rocky gorges where few bridges existed: the rare tracks were known only to local people. Apart from the châteaux of Antoine Laroche and Charles de Sauveterre, there were only a number of scattered farms, some isolated hamlets and the occasional village with a stone church.

The peasants were miserably poor and rarely had enough to eat, especially during the winter. And because they were totally uneducated and were surrounded by so much they could not understand, they lived in a state of constant fear.

When crops were blighted or oxen and sheep died, they knew it must be the work of some witch in league with the Devil. Fortunately for them the village priest usually helped to find the evil creature, very often an old woman. He handed her over to the Church, which forced her to repent before burning her as a warning to other evil-doers.

As well as witches, the peasants were afraid of the ghosts of evil-doers who returned from the grave to haunt them.

They feared too the wild animals in the dark forests, especially the savage wolves that descended from the heights in winter and prowled around the lonely farms and cottages in search of food.

Most of all they dreaded the *loup garou* – the werewolf – that creature of evil which it was almost impossible to kill and which lived on the flesh of men and women and children. At the time of the full moon, each peasant regarded his neighbour suspiciously, for it was then that a man might actually change into a wolf and stalk through the night in search of prey.

It was only a few minutes after Antoine Laroche left the château that the notary arrived. De Sauveterre insisted that what he wanted was more produce from his farms, longer hours of labour on his lands from every one of his peasants, and more money from all who possessed it in order to maintain the hospitality his position in society demanded.

The notary hesistated for a moment.

'May I remind Monsieur that the Church has the first claim of one tenth of the income or produce of every man on his estate, and draw to his attention the fact that many families are on the verge of starvation because of the failure of the crops this summer and the mysterious disease which has affected so many sheep and – ' He broke off, intimidated by the flush of anger on de Sauveterre's face. 'Very well, Monsieur, I will see what can be done.'

'I do not like this business of failed crops and sick animals,' de Sauveterre said curtly. 'It would apear to be the work of some witch who would ruin me and my family.'

The notary had his own ideas, but kept them to himself.

A whole day wasted, de Sauveterre thought, as he watched the notary ride off and then, seizing his velvet hat, he hurried through his grounds to the wood beyond, climbing the narrow path that he knew his friend must have taken some hours before.

It would be good to see Antoine again and hear what luck he had had. He would not have tried for a deer for that would be too heavy to carry back on his own. A hare perhaps. Or game birds.

The trees closed in on the path as it wound up the steep mountain side. He must tell his foresters to cut back the branches which had grown in spite of the summer drought. Why was it, he wondered, that crops which were needed failed, and tree branches which were just an obstruction, continued to grow?

Suddenly he halted.

Some distance away he could hear strange noises. Something was plunging through the forest, crashing against branches which snapped sharply. A wild boar or some other dangerous animal? What a fool he had been to have come out unarmed!

The noise was louder, nearer.

Whatever the animal, it was coming towards him.

He hunted for a weapon with which to defend himself and found only a fallen branch which broke in two between his hands.

It was too late to climb a tree. Now he could see something moving in that green gloom through which only the occasional shaft of fading sunlight penetrated – a bent figure, stumbling as though drunk and panting hoarsely . . . It was only when he was a few yards away that he recognized his friend.

'Antoine! What on earth is the matter? You run as though the Devil himself were pursuing you.'

'Charles! Thank heavens!' Fervently he grasped the other's hand. 'Let us flee from this place of danger as quickly as possible.' And he glanced over his shoulder and urged Charles on.

On both sides of the narrow track the trees whispered, dark and shadowy. Charles, following his friend, could see little of him, or indeed of himself, for from time to time he brought his hand up, peering at it because of some unpleasant stickiness, and then as the trees began to thin out and it grew lighter he saw that it was blood.

'Antoine – are you hurt? What has befallen you?'

'I will tell you everything once we are out of this wood. Quickly, my good friend. Quickly.'

He was still gasping for breath when they arrived in the grounds of the de Sauveterre estate, and there he turned and faced his friend.

'Antoine! What happened?'

Horrified, Charles stared at the long wounds which raked his friend's cheeks, at the holes torn in his leather doublet and padded trunks and hose and at the blood flowing from the savage wounds in his legs.

'I swear to you, Charles, I shall never set foot in that wood of yours again.' Antoine sat down on the grass and buried his still bleeding face in his hands. Seeing his distress, Charles waited, watching as the sun began to sink between the twin mountain peaks in the west.

At length Antoine looked up and began to speak, uneasily and jerkily, pausing frequently to draw a deep breath in an effort to regain control of himself.

'It was such a perfect day. I had no idea . . . no warning at all. I was striding along, whistling and stopping sometimes to listen for some sound that would betray a bird or perhaps a hare.

'And then it happened.

'Behind me.

'The sudden crashing of something leaping through the undergrowth where the trees are most dense and there is hardly any light at all. I half turned, but before I had time to raise my gun, a great beast,

21

snarling viciously, sprang at me, caught me off balance and I fell backwards.

'It was at my throat in an instant. Somehow, I do not know how, I got my hands round its neck and summoning up all my strength I hurled it to one side and staggered to my feet to face it.

'It was a wolf – but no ordinary beast. Bigger than any I have ever seen, its coat black as midnight and its wild eyes glaring at me with pure hatred.

'I remembered how you always maintained that to master a savage animal a man must meet its gaze steadily and without fear. Charles, at that moment I knew fear, but I think I hid it and I stared back into those terrible eyes for what seemed an eternity.

'Slowly the beast withdrew. And then it threw up its head and howled.

'You know what terror the howl of a wolf can strike in a man's heart at any time. This was ten times worse, for there was triumph and gloating in the drawn-out sound as well as an indefinable suggestion of something uncanny and evil.

'At that point my eyes must have betrayed my fear, for without warning the wolf sprang again.

'I defended myself as best as I could, using my gun to belabour it, but those long pointed claws gouged flesh from my face and legs and the fearful teeth worried at my clothes in a frenzy to reach the body underneath, and then the head moved up and the terrible jaws snapped at my throat again and tore the skin.

'When the beast knocked me to the ground a second time I knew there was only a faint chance of survival. I drew my hunting knife and struck out blindly, again and again and again. How I did it I do not know, but somehow I severed one of the creature's forepaws. The wolf howled in anguish, turned and made off, limping among the trees, while I scrambled to my feet and took to my heels.'

There was a long silence, broken only by Antoine's laboured breathing.

'The severed paw is in my hunting bag. Why I stopped to pick it up I have no idea, except that perhaps I thought I would have to convince myself later that somehow I had not imagined it all.

'See for yourself.' He opened his game bag. 'The paw is far bigger than that of any ordinary wolf, and as for its claws – ' He broke off and stared in horror at the object in his hand.

'Merciful heaven!' he cried, and both men crossed themselves in fear. For this was no animal's paw that he held.

It was the hand of a woman; the nails were pointed and encrusted with blood, while on the slender middle finger there was a magnificent emerald ring set with diamonds.

'Oh, no, no!' Charles de Sauveterre moaned, staring at the ring and then, very slowly he reached out and touched it with the tip of his forefinger, as though to assure himself of its reality.

'That ring,' he said hoarsely. 'I had it made specially for my wife a few weeks ago. The goldsmith swore there was not another like it in the whole of France. She . . . she thanked me so prettily and said she would treasure it above all the rest of her jewellery.'

'Your – your wife?'

Shocked and horrified the two men stared at each other and then Charles de Sauveterre spoke in a

23

strained voice, 'Stay where you are, Antoine. I shall send my men to help you.' And he raced back to the château.

'Pierre!' he shouted and as the servant hurried into the hall he asked, 'Your mistress – has she returned from her visit?'

'Yes, m'sieur. Madame returned a short while ago. She told Marie she was not well and retired to her bedroom to sleep. She said she was not to be disturbed on any account.'

Possessed by a terrible fear, Charles stared at the darkening stains on the marble floor of the hall and then he ran upstairs to his wife's room. The door was locked.

'Madame!' he shouted. 'Are you ill? Open this door! Open this door at once! It is I, your husband, who commands you!'

When there was no answer to his shouting and knocking, he called to Pierre to summon other servants to bring axes and break down the door, and as the lock yielded and everyone crowded into the doorway, from behind the closed curtains of the four poster bed there came a shrill cry of fear.

'Madame!' Charles de Sauveterre seized a candle from one of the maids, strode across the room and tore aside the curtains to gaze down at the blood-soaked sheets.

Slowly and with a trembling hand he turned back the top sheet and the colour fled from his cheeks as he stared at the hastily-improvised bandage.

'Madame has had an accident,' he said at length, and he replaced the sheet with care. 'Send for old Nou-nou quickly. She has great skill in attending to injuries, but' – he looked grimly at the servants – 'I do not think she has ever seen an injury like this.'

It was a pity that old Nou-nou was in time to save the life of the mistress of the château, for what was there for the poor lady to say when she was confronted with the evidence of her own severed hand with her ring on the middle finger?

Weeping, she confessed she had fallen under the spell of the evil Widow Bellenot who had taught her how to become a werewolf. 'Sir, if you will only let me depart I will enter a nunnery and spend my days in prayers and fasting. You must forget me and marry some lady worthy of you.'

'That I cannot do, for as long as you live, innocent people's lives will be at risk,' de Sauveterre said sternly, and sending for the priest, he handed his wife over to his care.

'First she must be questioned by magistrates,' the priest said, and though they interrogated her closely, she could not – or would not – tell them any more than her husband and Antoine Laroche had reported. And when officers went to arrest the Widow Bellenot, she had disappeared and was never seen in Auvergne again – which proved to some people that she was a witch.

'We find this woman to be indeed a werewolf,' the magistrates announced, 'and we hand her over to the protection of the Church.'

The Church protected her soul by tying her to a stake and burning her in the market place of the nearest town. And for possibly two or even three years no other werewolves were found in Auvergne.

3 Conn and the Other People

Long ago, on an island off the western coast of Erin, dwelt Cathal, a prosperous lord, with his young son, Conn, whom he loved dearly. Cathal was guided by Niall, the Druid, grey of hair and of beard, who was wise in all things past and much that was to come: by his learning and special gifts Niall protected the island, and all the peasants and fishermen who lived on it, from the evil and malice of The Other People, The Dispossessed Ones, the Banshees and Leprechauns who had once been all powerful in Erin but had been driven underground to live in the darkness of green hills and desolate boglands.

Because Cathal thought he should live as his people did, every day he worked with them, either as a farmer, or a fisherman in the dangerous Atlantic waters that surrounded his island, and as soon as Conn was old enough to sit astride a mule or take his place in a currach, he accompanied his father and learned how to win a living from both land and sea.

When Conn was five he accompanied his father, Niall and the chief men of the island to the nearest market town on Erin. With their surplus produce they went down to the one sandy beach protected by massive cliffs from winter storms and gales: here the fishermen beached their long currachs, and from here they crossed the strait to the stone harbour of the fishing hamlet on Erin.

Mules and donkeys awaited them, and they rode off to the market town where people gathered from all over the west coast to exchange and barter and buy what they could not make for themselves.

Conn grew up happily on the island, learning all the time from his father whom he loved and admired, from Niall the Druid whom he respected and regarded with awe, and from the peasants with whom he worked.

One market day, towards the end of his thirteenth year, he awoke with a slight fever and his father, after consulting the old Druid, decided it would be wiser if the lad remained in bed.

But at nightfall, when Niall and the others returned, Cathal was not with them.

'Your father has been detained by important business,' the old Druid told Conn. 'He will return in a few days, I assure you.' And he left the Big House and went to his sanctuary in a clearing in a grove of stunted oaks, and there he cast the Securable Rune for the safety of Cathal, and the Medicinal Rune for the recovery of Conn, and all throughout the dark night he recited the age-old wisdom of the Druids that had been passed on by word of mouth and never written down.

Within a few days Conn shook off his fever and worked and fished with the islanders as he had been taught, and though he wondered at his father's absence, he had such faith in him that he made no attempt to question Niall or any of the men who had been with him at the market on Erin.

A month after Cathal had left the island, the old Druid sent for Conn.

'Your father will return tomorrow at sunset. Let us go down to the beach and welcome him.'

But when Cathal returned he was not alone.

Beside him in his currach sat a beautiful raven-haired lady dressed in embroidered silks and velvet the like of which Conn had never seen before, for the island women wove their clothes from the natural wool of their own sheep. Behind them sat two lovely girls, as fair as the lady was dark, and just as richly dressed. A second, new currach followed the first: in this were tethered four fine Arab steeds, surrounded by many travelling cases.

Courteously Cathal handed out his three passengers and then, his arm round the lady with raven hair, he smiled proudly at his son.

'Conn, for long I have thought yours a lonely life here with me. A month ago I met this lady at the market on Erin and fell in love with her the moment I saw her. When I learned she was a widow, I courted her and yesterday we became man and wife. She has promised to care for you as I do. Salute your new mother, my son.'

Conn took the lady's gloved hand and bowed, but never, he thought, would he call this woman his mother.

'And my dear wife has brought her two daughters to be your sisters. Bid them welcome, Conn.'

Again Conn bowed, but made no effort to touch their gloved hands and secretly he vowed he would never regard them as kith or kin.

*

'As you have been absent for some time, do you wish to ride round the island tomorrow and see what work has been done, Father?' Conn asked during supper – a simple meal which pleased the stepmother little and her daughters not at all. 'There are several matters on which Niall and I would like your advice.'

'A ride first thing in the morning is exactly what I had in mind,' the stepmother cried, before Cathal could answer, and then she turned to Niall. 'It is thoughtless of my husband and son to overlook your age and expect you to gallop across the fields and rocks as they do. The time has come for you to rest and reflect. And as you leave us now, bid one of the servants have our four Arab steeds saddled and ready at first light.' Dismissing Niall, she smiled at Conn. 'When you are no longer a child you too shall have a fine horse.'

The next morning Cathal rode beside his wife, his attention all on her and not on the island or his people: her two daughters rode behind, laughing and talking in some strange language, and Conn rode alone on his mule with only his thoughts for company.

The following day, as Niall was discussing with Cathal repairs to some of the cottages, the new wife interrupted and put her arm through Cathal's, drawing him away.

'A lord as important as you should not concern himself with the day-to-day matters of the island. Niall and your servants can do that work. Why not enjoy life? Let us go hunting now for I saw some fine red deer in one of the woods yesterday.'

To this Cathal eagerly agreed, but Conn said he

29

had much to do and went off to work with Niall and the islanders as he had always done.

After that the daughters kept their own company, returning frequently to the mainland where they feasted and danced, but where and in what company no one knew. As for Cathal, so besotted was he by his new wife, that he spent all his time with her, caring little for his son and nothing for the old Druid or his island; and although Conn and Niall worked from sunrise to sunset they had neither the money nor the wherewithal to keep the land prosperous so that gradually a gread sadness spread over the people.

The day before Conn's fourteenth birthday, Niall, who no longer ate or slept at the Big House, drew Conn to one side.

'Would you trust me with your life and that of your father, Conn?'

'You know I would, Niall.'

'Then watch your stepmother carefully tonight at supper, for with her own hands she has prepared a special feast with costly wines. Say nothing of what you see to anyone, but at midnight when the moon is high over the Hill of the Cruel Dead, leave the house secretly and meet me behind the stable block. And – one word of warning! Drink only the milk to which you are accustomed and do not be persuaded to swallow even one drop of wine.'

'I will do as you say, Niall.'

The old Druid was already waiting behind the stable block when Conn arrived, breathless.

'What did you see, son of Cathal?'

'After my father's second wife failed to persuade me to drink anything but my customary milk, and while her daughters distracted him with some pleasantry, I saw her shake three drops of colourless liquid into my father's wine: presently he became drowsy and his new wife retired with him to bed.'

The old Druid sighed. 'It is as I feared. Your father sleeps a drugged sleep. Although I know what is about to happen, you must see for yourself. Follow me silently, for we must reach the top of the Hill of the Cruel Dead before they do.'

'I am frightened, Niall.' Conn shivered as he stared up at the seven massive upright stones and the great flat stone balanced on their tapering tips, silhouetted against the full moon. He remembered how people said that long ago a great chieftain had lived on the island: in his pride he had built himself a great hilltop tomb of hewn stones covered with turf and had arranged for all his tribe to attend a feast outside his tomb on the day he died. But secretly he had ordered his guard to slay the people, and his high priest to poison the guard, so that he should not go alone when he journeyed into the next world. Even the poisoner had died on the sword of a dying guard – so it was said – and ever since then the place had been accursed.

'Trust me, Conn,' the old Druid said, and together they climbed the steep winding track to the top of the Hill of the Cruel Dead, and Niall led the lad to a hollow fringed with reeds and covered with wild thyme: there they crouched, able to see the gaunt stones without being seen.

It was not long before they came.

Silently they glided across to the entrance of the burial mound, three tall forms clad in long black garments, dark veils hooding their heads, and there,

31

in that place of evil where so many had been killed, so much innocent blood shed, they knelt down and arms outstretched and palms flat on the earth, they kissed the ground.

Slowly they arose and where they had kissed the earth a flame flickered and a plume of smoke rose, swaying in the night wind. Joining hands the figures began to dance, the wind catching their veils and blowing them hither and thither, so that Conn, horrified, saw first one face and then another and recognized them. But they were not beautiful as he knew them, but white and gaunt, cheek bones protruding in the moonlight, sunken eyes now glittering, now blind, mouths black and terrifying cavities.

Presently they began to sing, very softly, a disquieting melody in some strange, eerie tongue.

As the dance quickened and the singing became more distracting, Niall touched Conn's arm, motioning to him to follow, and silently they stole away down the Hill of the Cruel Dead, past the Big House and down again to the sheltered beach where the currachs lay.

'Those women are The Other People, The Dispossessed, whom my father has brought to our island – is that not so, Niall?' Conn asked, trembling with fear and horror.

'That is so, Conn, son of Cathal.'

'They mean to enslave and kill my father with their evil powers and take over the island for themselves and their kind.'

'No, Conn. The one they mean to enslave and kill is not your father, but you. They know that their black arts are not so potent as my age-old learning when it comes to a battle over the body or the mind of a man. I can protect your father, but there is little in our lore to protect a youth.

'Tonight I watched them begin the first spell to draw the soul from your body: and I knew I had no counter charm. You must leave the island now, telling no one, not even your father.'

As he spoke he was untying a light coracle, gesturing to Conn to help him drag it down to the sea and ship the oars.

'When we reach the fishing hamlet at the far side of the strait, follow the track along the river and climb up into the mountains of Erin. There is bread for you in this leather bag that will last for five days. Find yourself a place as a shepherd and work there until the day you are twenty one and a man.'

'I cannot leave my father and my people for seven long years,' Conn cried in anguish.

'Trust my magic. I shall see they come to no harm. And I promise you this, if you remember all your father and I and your people have taught you, you will return to claim the island and rule it wisely.'

The moon had disappeared and the stars were pale when they pulled into the mainland harbour. Sadly Conn embraced the old Druid, watched him turn back, and then, with a heavy heart, he set off past the sleeping stone huts of the fishermen of Erin, to follow the stony track that led high into the mountains.

For four days he journeyed, avoiding farms, hamlets and lone shepherds, and sleeping in the heather and bracken. On the fifth morning he came to a farm that had an air of recent neglect although it was obviously still occupied.

Round to the yard at the back he walked where he

33

saw a farmer and a girl of his own age struggling to mend a broken plough.

'You need help with that,' he said, and in a short while the work was done and he had learned that a sickness had plagued the district: the farmer and his daughter, Deidre, had had to take to their beds, and the hired men, expecting them to die and afraid for their own lives, had run off without telling anyone.

At once Conn offered his services as shepherd, ploughman and general handyman, and though he was but a lad, the farmer, with his daughter's approval, hired him at once.

There was so much to be done that Conn, knowing he need not worry about the island or his father as the old Druid would take good care of them, put to work all the skills and knowledge he had already learned.

As the months and years passed the farm prospered, fresh help was hired, and the farmer looked on Conn almost as a son, but Deidre had ideas of her own.

At length, three days before his twenty-first birthday, Conn told Deidre what had happened before he came to Erin, and confessed that he had loved her secretly all the seven years he had worked on the farm.

'Would you marry me, Deidre, and when the time comes, journey with me and live in my island home?'

As Deidre had long loved Conn, she accepted him immediately: they sought out her father who gave his consent to the betrothal and together they arranged for the marriage to take place after the harvest.

But that evening, as they sat talking round the fire, a stranger knocked at the door.

'Are you that Conn, son of Cathal, who left his island home off the west coast of Erin seven years past?'

'I am that Conal.'

'Then I am come to you from Niall the Druid to bid you return on your twenty-first birthday, when you are a man, if you are to save your father's life.' Unable to give any more information and refusing refreshment, the stranger turned and walked away.

Naturally Deirdre was distressed and feared for Conn's safety, as she knew of The Other People, The Dispossessed Ones, and the harm they still caused in other kingdoms in Erin; but she hid her fears.

'Your duty is to your father as I am not yet your wife. Ride your favourite black stallion and we shall pray for you night and morning, my father and I.'

Embracing her, Conn set off over the mountains and through the glens and on the day before his twenty-first birthday he rode down the track to the fishing hamlet on the rocky western coast of Erin.

To his dismay, all was changed. There were no currachs tied up in the harbour and all the stone huts were deserted. From only one dwelling came the drift of peat smoke, but the door was closed, the window shuttered.

'Good Kathleen, let me in. It is I, Conn, son of Cathal, returning to my island home. Many a time have you dandled me on your knee and fed me on goats' milk and honey cakes. Open your door for me, Kathleen.'

Slowly the wooden bars on the door were drawn, slowly the door opened and an old woman peered out.

'Ochone! Ochone!' she wept. 'It is indeed Conn, son of Cathal. But surely you are come too late.'

'What has happened, Kathleen? How is my father? And Niall? And all the fisher folk who used to live here?'

'I know nothing of the island and its people now. All I can tell you is that for long Niall the Druid used his ancient arts to protest us. So wise and learned was he that the three women from The Other People, The Dispossessed Ones, were powerless against him. As they could not find out the place of safety to which the Druid had sent you, they could not use your youthful dreams to work their evil magic, or turn your love for your father against his people.

'But Niall was old and the seven long years took their toll of him: his magic weakened as did his health, yet he dared not send for you until you were a man.

'At last the three evil ones turned his runes against him. Fishermen drowned even when the waters of the straits were calm. Fever swept through the island and this hamlet, and those who survived fled. But I remained here, knowing that when the time was come, you would surely return and drive out the Evil Ones and save us.'

'I must cross to the island at once and find out what has happened to my father and Niall. Where can I find a currach?'

'Only the Ferryman crosses the strait in safety now: anyone else drowns. Stable your black stallion with me and I will care for it until – if – you return.' And she closed the door and would not open it in spite of his entreaties.

He stabled his horse and walked to the rocky shore, unhappy in the thought that perhaps it was his love for Deidre that had helped to weaken Niall's magic, and yet he knew it was a love that had come of its own accord, and because he had held it secret within him for seven years, not once had he imagined it might be used against his father or the old Druid.

Never before had there been a Ferryman between Erin and the island, and why there should be one now when the hamlet was deserted, he could not guess, and whether this Ferryman was good or evil, he had no means of knowing.

Nevertheless he clambered along the rocky coast until at last he came to a cottage standing by itself in a little bay, a currach drawn up on the pebbly beach.

Knocking on the door he looked proudly at the man who answered, for if Conn was now tall and broad and strong, the Ferryman was taller and stronger and broader, and if Conn was dark of hair and beard, this man was darker still, and his countenance was fierce and grim.

'Are you the Ferryman?' Conn asked.

'I am, stripling,' the Ferryman answered.

'Guard your tongue, Ferryman, for I am Conn, son of Cathal, and I will pay you well to take me over the strait to my father's island.'

'I take no stripling over the strait by daylight, for he will surely drown, though I myself will return.'

'Then take me at midnight, for then it will be dark and I shall have attained manhood.'

'So be it. Come when the first of the Merry Dancers colours the midnight sky and I and my currach will be ready.'

And the Ferryman slammed shut his door.

Mustering both his patience and his courage Conn went down to the shore, found a flat rock, ate the last of the food Deirdre had given him, stretched himself out and fell fast asleep.

*

When he awoke dim stars shone in the dark sky and then, far to the north a great cone of light appeared, soaring and pulsating, and from it crimson, azure, green and purple streamers quivered and glowed, stretching and soaring upwards through the stars to an amber crown.

As Conn turned his gaze from the sky he saw the Ferryman had launched his currach and was waiting for him.

'Have you the courage to face the power of The Other People, The Dispossessed Ones, O Conn, son of Cathal, who was but a stripling when he knocked on my door some hours back but has, with the passing of midnight, become a man?'

'I have,' Conn said steadfastly.

The Ferryman pointed to the sky where the Northern Lights (which some out of fear and to placate what they could not understand called the Merry Dancers) had dissolved and reformed so that the whole of the sky to the north was red.

Blood red.

'Are you a warrior and versed in swordsmanship?'

Conn shook his head.

'I am a farmer and fisherman and have always been a man of peace, but my heart is as stout as any warrior's if I must fight evil.'

'Then take this.' And the Ferryman gave Conn a great double-edged sword that gleamed scarlet in the pagan splendour of the blood-red sky. 'And cut the waves as they come.'

'But there is not a breath of wind and the strait is as calm as a millpond,' Conn protested.

'Sit in the prow,' the Ferryman said, ignoring Conn's protest, 'and speak no word. Three waves will

38

come out of the calmness and unless you cut them they will sink you and the currach and that will be the end of you and all you hold dear.'

Conn stepped into the currach and took his seat at the prow and waited.

They were half-way across the strait when from nowhere a great wave rose up, towering high ahead of them: immediately Conn bent forwards over the prow and cut it, and the wave turned dark and fell back and died. And the Ferryman rowed safely on.

It was not long before a second great wave rose up, towering even higher than the first, and Conn leaned forward and cut it, so that it fell back and died. And the Ferryman rowed safely on.

As they were nearing the island the third wave arose, greater, more terrifying than the others, and Conn's eyes glittered and his mouth was grim as he leaned far out over the prow, swung his sword mightily with both hands and cut the wave. And it fell back and died. And the Ferryman rowed the currach to the island beach just as the Merry Dancers faded away and left the sky to the pale stars.

'What is your fare, Ferryman?' Conn asked.

'You have paid that already, Conn, son of Cathal,' the Ferryman answered, taking back the sword and placing it beside him; and even as Conn jumped out, he turned and rowed into the dark night.

Up the rocky track Conn ran and across to the Big House, and there at the open door sat Niall the Druid: where his hair had been grey, now it was white, and there were tears streaming down his cheeks.

'My ancient magic was powerful,' he whispered, as Conn knelt and put his arms round the old man, 'but my life force ebbed with the passing of time. When

39

the seventh year was nearly ended I summoned you with the last of my powers to put an end to the evil of The Other People, The Dispossessed Ones.'

'My father?'

'He is frail but now he will recover his wits and his strength. Go into the House and there you will see what you will see. My work is done, O Conn, who left as a boy and returned as a man. Now I can go in peace to join my forefathers and the Druids of old.'

And he closed his eyes, and no breath came from his mouth.

Conn kissed Niall's brow and then strode into the House.

In the first room lay the bodies of his stepmother and step-sisters in their black hooded garments, each body cut in half as if by a great double-edged sword, each consisting only of dry and brittle bones. And he knew that at last he had freed the island from The Other People who had bewitched his father.

Once it was known that Conn had put an end to the evil Other People, peasants and fishermen returned to the island and the coast of Erin.

Although Cathal recovered his health, he knew himself to be too old to rule the island he had so long neglected. 'Return to your farm and marry Deirdre,' he told Conn.

'Bring her back with you and together you will make the island a happy and prosperous place again, for Niall has ensured with his last runes and spells that never more will it be troubled by The Other People, The Dispossessed Ones.'

4   The Norwegian Monsters

Many centuries ago there lived in Norway two warriors named Sigmund and Sinfjöth, men of great
energy and great physical endowment.

In their youth they sailed in open boats with
companions in search of adventure and fame and
treasure, and they landed on many strange islands
and in many different countries: sometimes they found
perpetual snow and ice, sometimes rain and fog and a
dampness which chilled them to the bone, but on
occasion they found places where the sun shone and
the grass was green and food abundant.

Although they met no one who could speak their
language, there were those who fed them and made
them welcome: other men in other places greeted
them with war cries and swords and battle axes, and
blood was spilt and men died, both Norsemen and
strangers alike.

Often the cold grey sea, its towering waves seven
times higher than the tallest man, plunged and fell on
the dragon-prowed ships, claiming the lives of Norsemen when they were returning with their booty. They
had snatched golden crosses adorned with precious
stones from some strange house of worship they had
set on fire. There were twisted torcs of gold from the
necks of dying chieftains, rings and brooches, brace-

lets and clasps of gold and spoons and bowls of engraved silver.

But the Norse gods smiled on Sigmund and Sinfjöth. Both were wounded more than once and indeed Sigmund was to limp to the end of his days from the mighty swing of a Saxon battle axe which had nearly severed his right leg above the knee.

But whether it was in battle with men or with monsters, or whether it was fighting the gales and the might of the seas, neither warrior ever knew one single moment of fear.

The youthful years passed. The desire for adventure and excitement was satisfied. Although much treasure had come their way, they always seemed to lose it again, in battle or pleasure, by accident or theft, or in games of chance and reckless gambling, so that when after many years they sailed back to Norway they were no richer than when they left, except of course in experience of the ways of mankind.

'The gods have looked after us in our youth,' Sigmund said. 'They will surely look after us now.'

And the gods were kind – at first.

Sigmund gambled all he possessed in the first port at which they landed and won from a simple-minded peasant his single-roomed hut and small strip of barren windswept land. By further gambling and skilful cheating and by bartering the two became the joint owners of a rich, well-stocked farm on one of the fjords to the far north where, they were assured, the fishing and the hunting were all a Norseman could desire.

*

'We must have someone to cook for us and to see to the management of the house,' Sinfjöth said, when they reached their farm and found it all they had dreamed of when they had travelled and fought in foreign lands.

'We shall enquire of the head man in the settlement nearby,' Sigmund said. 'Perhaps he can tell us of some widow who would care for us in return for a roof over her head and food to keep her alive.'

Greatly to their surprise, however, they found that the head of the settlement was not a man but a woman, a Viking widow tall and strong enough to have been a warrior herself.

There is nore sagacity in this woman than in many a warrior, Sinfjöth thought, but he kept this thought to himself and as usual let Sigmund do most of the talking.

The head woman listened to their request, questioned Sigmund about their travels and ocean voyages and even more closely about their plans for the future and considered his answers carefully.

'My daughter will come and work for you,' she said at length. 'She has been brought up in my household and I know her to be a capable housewife and a good cook.

'See that no harm comes to her under your roof, for if any man lays as much as a finger on her he will pay with his life, for I have many kinsmen who will hunt him down, even though he flees to the very edge of the world.'

Hastily Sigmund swore that no harm would come to her daughter and Sinfjöth assured her the girl would be as safe under their roof as under that of her mother.

'And now that it would appear your roving years are over, warriors, and that you propose to spend the remainder of your time here with us, see to it that you do not offend the spirits of the river or the forests or the high mountains, and have a respect for the goods and property of others.'

Again Sigmund swore that they would heed what she had advised.

'One last word, warriors,' she said, before she summoned her daughter – who was listening eagerly behind the door in the next room. 'In the forests which line the fjord hereabouts there dwell certain malevolent beings – sorcerers and enchanters – who can induce in the bravest heart a fear so powerful that ultimately it drives a man to kill what he holds most dear and then to take his own life. Therefore take heed that neither of you commits any careless or untoward act which would place you in the power of such malevolent ones.'

The girl, who was young and exceedingly beautiful, was well pleased to have the care of the rich farm and the two warriors, and Sigmund and Sinfjöth rejoiced and congratulated themselves on their good fortune. As throughout the many dangers of their adventurous lives they had never known a single moment of fear, they assured each other they need not concern themselves with the malevolent ones of the forests, and so they quickly forgot all about them.

When they were not working on the farm, Sigmund and Sinfjöth fished for salmon and trout in the waters of the fjord, or hunted among the spruce and firs growing high on the steep mountain-sides and brought back in triumph hare and wolverene, elk and reindeer and bear.

During the long dark winter months when there was no sun at all they sat by the fire and talked of old friends and magnificent exploits, but when the girl told them it was the time of the Merry Dancers, the Northern Lights, they pulled on their furs and joined the others in the settlement, hunting and breaking the thick ice to fish, and feasting, as the old gods lit up the sky with many coloured lights so that it was as bright as a summer's day, and everyone sang and rejoiced until the colours faded and darkness settled again on the fjord.

They had lived contentedly enough on the farm for nearly a year when one morning Sigmund, who had begun to show certain signs of restlessness, turned to his friend.

'Do you think that perhaps the time has come for us to find wives and have sons like us – and daughters too?'

Sinfjöth gave the matter thought.

'How would we find wives?' he asked.

'I would not mind making the girl my wife,' Sigmund answered casually. 'She is strong and healthy and an excellent cook.'

Sinfjöth gave this reply even more thought, while in the kitchen the girl listened eagerly behind the door.

'The girl is kind and beautiful too. I should consider myself the most fortunate of men if she would marry me,' he said at length.

As it was obvious that both could not marry the same girl – and neither thought to ask her opinion – they agreed to abandon the idea for the time being, and taking up their knives and spears they set off to hunt in a forest in which they had not previously set foot.

Higher they climbed and higher through the spruce and firs without catching sight of a single animal: hungrier and hungrier they grew, and just when they decided they would have to turn and go back empty-handed for the very first time, they came to a clearing in which stood a small wooden cabin.

'Let us hope the owner is at home and can offer us some refreshment,' Sinfjöth said, and he knocked on the door.

From inside there came only the sound of heavy snoring.

Again Sinfjöth knocked and again, but the snoring continued loudly and regularly.

'This man would sleep through the Twilight of the Gods and the End of the World,' Sigmund cried, and elbowing his friend to one side he flung open the door and stared into the gloomy interior. On the floor two men slept and snored under warm coverings of furs and hides, and not all the shouting and shaking of the warriors could waken them.

'They must have been hunting for seven days at least to be so tired,' Sigmund said.

'Nine days,' Sinfjöth corrected, and then wondered how he had known this.

'And what skill they must have to kill two such fine beasts,' Sigmund continued, looking not at the bear and reindeer skins which covered the sleeping hunts-men, but at the splendid wolfskins hanging on the wall, the grey fur thick and long and silken-tipped. 'Such wolfskins would keep a man warm indeed in the bitter winter days when the sun forgets to rise.' He stared at the pelts with admiration and envy. 'This one would fit you to perfection.' Stretching his arm above one of the snoring huntsmen, he lifted the wolfskin off the wooden peg on the wall and threw it to Sinfjöth, and then helped himself to the second skin.

Snugly each warrior fitted first his legs and then his arms and body and last of all his head into the splendid wolfskin, but just as each opened his mouth to express his delight at the warmth of the fur which might have been made especially for him, he suddenly felt himself to be trapped.

In vain they struggled to tear off those furs and free themselves: in vain they tried to shout for help, to ask each other what was happening. Suddenly each was aware that some diabolical influence had taken over and they must live for ever in the wolfskins and now, instead of speaking, they could only howl.

And for the first time in their lives Sigmund and Sinfjöth knew fear for as they looked at each other they saw they were men no longer.

They were werewolves, the most foul and accursed monsters in Norway.

For a moment they stood there, paralysed by terror, and then dropping on all fours they stared at the sleeping hunters. Terror gave way to rage as animal instincts prevailed: sharp blue eyes were now black with fury and wide jaws opened to reveal cruel teeth as the creatures prepared to leap on their victims and devour them to satisfy their terrible hunger.

But the huntsmen, wakened by those first agonised howls, had already realized their danger. Together they flung the bearskins and hides at the wolves, almost smothering them, and belaboured them frantically with clubs until they leaped from the cabin and disappeared among the trees of the dark forest.

Enraged by the escape of their victims, the warrior-wolves turned on each other, snarling and biting, howling and tearing at fur and flesh, muscle and bone, until, exhausted and blood-stained and filled again with fear because they were unable to understand how they had been changed from men to monsters, they slunk back through the forest and down to their farmhouse.

When the girl saw the two great werewolves approaching the door, she slammed it shut immediately, and although they howled and snarled the livelong night in the bitter cold, leaping high at the shuttered windows and scratching wildly at the door, she refused to open it to them.

At last, hungry and shivering and possessed by a fearful nameless dread, Sigmund and Sinfjöth sought the shelter of an empty barn, and each choosing a corner as far from the other as possible, licked his wounds and fell asleep.

When they awoke the girl was standing in the doorway with her mother, the Viking widow and the head of the settlement. Immediately the hungry were-wolves sprang up, snarling and howling, and would have attacked them both had not the widow spoken to them sharply in some almost forgotten language while at the same time she made over each the sign of the cross. Slowly the evil and anger which had possessed them ebbed away and they lay down again, watching her with mournful eyes in which fear and terror still lurked.

First the head woman bade her daughter fetch fresh water and newly-caught salmon, and when she knew the hungry beasts had satisfied their hunger and thirst, she spoke, slowly and gravely.

'Sigmund and Sinfjöth, you are werewolves now and no longer warriors.' The monstrous creatures shuddered and closed their eyes, unable to meet the fierce stare of the Viking widow. 'You can understand what I say but you cannot speak.'

Sigmund lifted his head and struggled to say he was the one to blame but all he could achieve was a melancholy howling which filled him with horror.

'When you first came to live here I warned you of the malevolent beings that dwell in the dark forests and I warned you not to commit any careless or untoward act which might place you in their power.

'High up among the tall spruce and firs there lives a sorcerer who, in the time of our forefathers, was cast out from amongst us because of the evil he wrought.

'He hates mankind and his spells are powerful and binding on those who have killed or stolen or committed any crime.'

The werewolves were still, remembering fleetingly their warrior lives when they had been proud to fight and kill and steal.

'The last time I saw those grey wolfskins, the fur so thick and long and silken-tipped, they were worn by two robbers who had tried to kill the sorcerer while he slept. There and then he turned them into werewolves, and when they crawled to me for help, knowing I am versed in the ancient magic, all I could offer them was that for one day in every ten they might become men again. But so exhausting and so dangerous is the life of a werewolf that they were forced to spend that one day asleep while gaining strength for the next nine.

'In stealing those wolfskins, you have released the robbers, but you have taken the spell on yourselves. You are werewolves now – monsters, and no longer warriors.'

The werewolves stood up and howled in anguish and then shrank back in their dark corners, for though they had the bodies of animals, they had the thoughts of men and they were ashamed and afraid because they did not know what would become of them.

Seeing their despair, the girl turned and pleaded with her mother.

'Sigmund and Sinfjöth are heroes, not robbers, and it is by accident and not by design that now they are werewolves. Our settlement needs such warriors as these. You and only you can undo the evil of the sorcerer.'

The mother looked at her daughter, knowing that the time would come when she would have to pass on her ancient skills and knowledge so that the girl could take her place as head of the settlement. And then there must be yet another generation to learn the secrets of the old wisdom. Her daughter must marry. Better a live warrior husband than a dead Viking hero, she thought, and sighed deeply.

'Some part of this I can do,' she said, 'but the warriors themselves must do more.' She turned to the cowering, fearful monsters, who were neither wolf nor man. 'For nine days you must remain as you are. During that time, lest you be tempted to fight or to kill according to the wolf's nature, you must remain shut up in the darkness of this barn where food and water will be brought to you daily.

'You will be tempted to attack both the bringer of the food and each other.

'If, by the tenth day, you have restrained yourselves according to the code of mankind, then the wolfskins will drop away and you will be warriors once again and welcomed back into the settlement as heroes.'

For nine days the werewolves slept as animals and wakened and forced themselves to think as men, but each time the girl appeared with water and fish or meat some form of rivalry which they could not understand urged them to attack each other and fight to the death. Always however, first one and then the other controlled himself and drew back snarling and growling.

When at long last the tenth day arrived, they awoke suddenly, stepped from their wolfskins and ran rejoicing out of the barn into the sunlight, where the head woman and her daughter awaited them.

After thanking the widow for saving them from the dreadful fate which might have been theirs, they followed her advice, gathered up the hated skins, burned them and threw the ashes into the fjord, where they floated for a moment on the swift current and then sank to be lost for ever in the dark, cold waters.

After this, they both turned to the girl and asked her if she would marry one of them and find a wife for the other.

She readily agreed, and much to Sigmund's surprise, chose Sinfjöth for her husband. Soon Sigmund married another girl from the settlement and all four lived happily together on the farm.

Long afterwards, when their sons had sailed on many voyages as Viking warriors and had returned home and settled down, their children delighted to sit by their grandfathers, listening to one particular tale over and over again, so that they in their turn would be able to pass on to their grandchildren the story of how once the warriors Sigmund and Sinfjöth had gone into the dark forest as men and returned as werewolves, and how for nine days they lived with a fear more terrible then any warrior could know on the battlefield or when he was storm-tossed and at the mercy of the great waves in his dragon-prowed ship.

5   The Phantom Bride

Alexis awoke abruptly, propping himself up on one arm to stare around the unfamiliar room. What had happened to bring him to this place?

Bewildered, he watched the sunlight stream through the window, and then as the door began to open he remembered the whole nightmare journey and he stared at the burly, bearded man who entered.

'Good morning, my dear Count. I trust you slept well? I regret I was not here to receive you and the Countess when you arrived at our village last night.' The stranger, who spoke excellent Russian, looked closely at Alexis's eyes and face and then threw back the bedclothes to examine his bruised legs and blistered feet. 'Here I am called Father Peter as I am priest to this little village, though I am the doctor as well. Although you could not understand the peasants' tongue or they your Russian one, they could see you were in need of food and shelter.'

'Yes, Father Peter. They were indeed kind and hospitable. How is the Countess Natalia?'

'I have just come from seeing her at the Widow Anna's cottage. She is suffering from exhaustion and has a slight fever. She would do well to stay in bed for two or three days.' He looked up as a young girl stood hesitantly in the doorway. 'Come in, child. Put our breakfast on the table and thank your mother from both of us.

'And while we eat, dear Count, perhaps you can tell me how you and your charming Countess stumbled on this remote village in an almost forgotten area of Mother Russia.'

'We have been dogged by ill fortune,' Alexis explained to Father Peter as they ate the black bread, cheese and hard-boiled eggs. 'After staying with the Countess Natalia's family we set off on a long-promised visit to my parents in Moscow. But soon disaster struck. Such inns as there were, were run by rogues: where there were no inns the post houses were filthy. The countess's maid fell sick and we had to arrange for her to be cared for and sent home.

'When we set off again we followed a track through a forest but somehow took the wrong turning and it was dark before we realized we were hopelessly lost. Rather than return to that last post house we rode on, assuring each other that at any moment we would find somewhere to rest. But there was nowhere – not even a cottage or hut. And of course we had no food.

'Then Natalia's horse stumbled and threw her. Fortunately she was not injured, but the horse had broken its leg. I had to shoot it.

'We slept underneath a tree and the next day discarded most of our luggage and Natalia rode on my horse and I walked.

'And so we continued for three whole days.

'We were weak with hunger and just when Natalia confessed that she had not the strength to ride any farther I smelt wood smoke and – as you said – stumbled on your village, and how I shall ever thank those good people for coming to our rescue, I do not know.'

'I have thanked them on your behalf. Now, as soon as you are ready I shall take you to call on the countess and satisfy yourself that everything possible has been done for her.'

And Natalia, so warmly covered in woollen blankets, her long dark hair loose on the pillow, her brown eyes drowsy in her pale oval face, had indeed been well cared for. Father Peter smiled down at her, spoke briefly to the Widow Anna, who immediately arose and followed him out of the one-roomed cottage, and now the two lovers were left alone.

'I shall soon be quite well, my beloved,' Natalia insisted, seeing the concern on Alexis's face. 'Although I remember very little of how we got here, I know the Widow Anna has been very kind to me. This must be her bed, for last night she slept in the straw in the corner by the door.'

'Probably where she keeps her sheep and geese during the winter,' Alexis said.

'Perhaps. But she brought me cool drinks when I was fevered and restless, brushed my hair and sang to me what must have been some kind of lullaby, so that at last I fell asleep.

'But, Alexis, what have you told Father Peter about us?'

'The truth – almost.'

'Not – not that we are eloping?'

'Of course not. Nor did I mention that we are most certainly being pursued by your father and brothers. But where once I thought we were plagued by ill luck, now I think fortune has smiled on us to lead us to this village where no one can possibly find us.

55

'Will you be content to stay here for a few days, my darling?'

'Indeed I will, Alexis. It is all so clean and cared for.' Pausing, she looked at him anxiously. 'But our stay will be only for a few days, I trust? For so long I have dreamed of the time when we should stand together in the Cathedral of St Basil in Moscow, you in your splendid uniform and I in my white bridal gown and when at last we are pronounced man and wife, no one shall keep us apart.'

'It will only be for a few days. I promise you that, Natalia.'

That evening Alexis brought up the subject of payment for their food and lodging, but Father Peter shook his head and smiled.

'We have no use for Russian money here. We live simply by hunting and fishing: we watch over our few sheep and cattle, goats and geese for they are necessary for our survival: we grow corn and vegetables and when necessary we exchange and barter goods.'

'My horse?'

'Is stabled next door and will pasture with mine.'

'I am indeed grateful, Father Peter, but as soon as Natalia is well we must continue our journey. And for that I must have a second horse.'

'Mine is the only horse in the village and that I need when I am called out to distant hamlets – as I was last night when you arrived.

'In two weeks' time, however, the gypsies will call to trade with us. One of them will certainly have horses to sell and I shall be there to see you are not cheated.'

Under the Widow Anna's care Natalia grew

stronger daily until, leaning on the old woman's arm, she ventured out into the spring sunshine and walked around the village square, smiling as the women curtseyed to her and the men bowed. The next day she walked with Alexis down to the chattering river and there they rested, looking back to the dense forests which protected the little settlement.

One morning Father Peter put on a long, full-skirted black cassock, placed round his neck a gold chain from which hung a gold cross, and celebrated mass in the wooden church next door. All the villagers attended: they wore their worn working clothes although some of the women had put on clean aprons and shawls: the short service over, they all returned immediately to their labours.

'It is a simple service which I inherited from my predecessor many years ago,' Father Peter commented, as he too put away the signs of his office. 'The peasants like it but what my superiors in Moscow would say about it I prefer not to think.' He put his hand on Alexis's shoulder and smiled. 'It was good to see two young faces in my flock of middle-aged and elderly people. What the future holds for them I do not know.'

Early the next morning the Widow Anna knocked on the door and called out in an anxious voice.

'Her cow is calving, Count Alexis,' Father Peter said. 'I am needed.'

It was not until Alexis returned to go to bed that evening that he saw Father Peter again, looking tired and concerned.

'The calf was born dead. The cow has some kind of infection but what it is I do not know. We have taken the other beasts to a fresh pasture by the river, but they have little appetite. If anything happens to them we shall have only goats' milk and that will not be enough for our survival.

'I do not understand it, Count Alexis. All the animals spend the cruel winter months in the cottages: the very old peasants sleep beside them for warmth. It is terrible to lose something as precious and necessary as a cow just when spring has come.

'I know more than anyone here about the ailments of our animals but I cannot understand why that cow died.'

'Another cow died today,' Natalia said when Alexis joined her for supper the next evening.

'How do you know? Did Father Peter tell you? I have not seen him all day.'

'No. The Widow Anna. I could tell from the expression on her face and her gestures. Oh, Alexis, these simple people live on the very edge of poverty and I feel we should not be here eating their precious food when they have so little.'

'When the gypsy traders come, my beloved, I will buy what beasts I can from them and give them to Father Peter for the peasants.'

'That is a splendid idea, Alexis. Tell him tonight so that it will comfort him a little.'

But the priest did not return to his cottage that night, and the following morning, when Alexis met him briefly in the square, he learned that all the cows had died and now the infection had spread to the goats.

Neither he nor Natalia had any appetite for their evening meal, and when he took his leave of her they stood for a moment at the open door, looking out at the square where the peasants were gathered arguing in low voices, glancing fearfully around, sometimes over to the dark forest, sometimes down to the river and then up to the cloud-swept sky.

They feel defenceless against the forces that exist around them, Natalia thought as she undressed and climbed into bed, and when much later she heard the Widow Anna return and sigh deeply as she made up the fire to last through the night, she lay still and pretended to be asleep.

But sleep would not come.

In the dark corner beside the door the old woman breathed heavily and evenly, but tonight there seemed to be something different about the room with which Natalia had grown familiar, a feeling which made her so uneasy that at last she sat up and stared about her in the dim firelight.

Suddenly she caught her breath as a figure moved silently from the shadows and stood in front of the fire – a girl dressed in white, a garland of flowers in her long dark hair.

'Who are you?' Natalia whispered. 'How did you get in here? What do you want?'

Motionless the girl stared at the fire but now it seemed to Natalia that the room was gradually suffused with a stronger, eerie light, so that she could see the gown the girl wore was of fine linen, delicately embroidered, quite unlike the coarse material of the peasant women.

'What a lovely dress,' she said softly. 'It is beautiful enough to be a bridal gown.'

Slowly the girl turned round so that Natalia could

see her face, her lips parted, her eyes wide with fear, and then she saw the dark sinister stain where the dress curved under the girl's left breast.

'You are wounded! What has happened? Speak to me. Tell me what has happened to you.' That stain, was it slowly spreading or was it some trick of the unearthly light? 'Let me help you – or the Widow Anna. Yes, she will know what to do.'

'I want to rest.' The words came falteringly from the pale lips and then the girl lifted her right arm and an expression of desperate entreaty came over her face as she pointed to the roof beam above. 'Please look . . . but do not tell . . .'

In the corner the straw rustled as the Widow turned: at the sound the girl vanished and the strange light faded.

The Widow Anna continued to breathe evenly and heavily.

Shivering, Natalia peered around, searching for the terrified visitor. The door had remained barred all the time and so she could not have come in or left by it. Had she dreamed it all? But surely people did not dream when they were awake and fully conscious? Perhaps – and she sighed and lay down – she was feverish again and had simply imagined the entreaty on that pale face and those hesitating words.

Presently she fell into such a deep sleep that she did not hear the Widow Anna rise, place the wooden yoke with the two dangling buckets across her shoulders and go off to the well for the day's water: and Alexis had to shake her gently before, much later, she awoke.

'The peasants are worried and uneasy,' he said. 'No work is being done. Everyone is afraid.'

'I too am afraid,' Natalia said. And she told him

how she had awakened to find a girl in a white dress bathed in a strange light, a frightened girl who had wanted to rest but had said only a few words before disappearing.

'A girl in a white dress, my beloved, in this village?'

'Yes. Do not laugh at me, Alexis, but I am convinced now that she did not exist as you and I do. I think she was a phantom . . . a phantom bride.'

'Of course I shall not laugh at you, my Natalia. But you have had a fever, and might it not be that perhaps you were dreaming of our wedding, of yourself in your bridal dress?' And he kissed the palm of her hand.

'That is what I told myself. But I am uneasy and so, to set my mind at rest, close the door so no one can see in and then reach up to that beam in front of the fireplace. There was such a look of entreaty on her face when she said "Please," that I am convinced she wanted to tell me something of great importance.'

Alexis did as she asked and as his fingers groped along the beam they encountered something bulky: grasping this with both hands he lifted it down – a strangely-shaped cloth bundle, the ends knotted together.

'You open it,' Natalia begged, and she watched as he undid the knots and unfolded the cloth and then she gave a strangled gasp as he picked up an elongated bleached skull.

'It is only a sheep's head,' he said reassuringly. 'But why should anyone want to keep this?'

Natalia now was more concerned with the garment which lay beneath the skull. Lifting it gently, she shook it out of its folds and placed it in front of her on the bed, and they both stared, unbelievingly, at a white embroidered bridal gown which had been most carefully washed and pressed.

Slowly Natalia's fingers traced the faint stain where it had fitted over the bride's breast and then stopped, trembling. Now they could both see, at the top of the stain, that the fabric had been cut by some sharp instrument and then the edges had been sewn together with uneven stitches.

'What does it mean?' Natalia asked fearfully.

'Fold it up again,' Alexis urged. 'Exactly as it was. Quickly, before the Widow Anna returns.' And when the bundle was back in its original hiding place he kissed her gently. 'Get up and dress but remain here. I must ask Father Peter for an explanation.'

The minute he went out into the square he could sense a change in the mood of the peasants. The family groups had split up and all the women were gathered outside the barn where the grain was stored each autumn: they were curiously excited and pleased about something, and every now and again one would turn and shout out to the men, giving orders in a tone of authority quite unlike her usual manner of speaking.

'What is happening? Why is everyone so different?' he asked, as Father Peter hurried across to him. 'Has the sickness been checked?'

'On the contrary. There is little hope for any of the goats. You must tell the Countess to remain in her cottage until we return.'

'Rturn? Why, where are we going?'

'Hunting. Go and tell her now and I will explain later when we are alone. Act naturally and do not draw attention to yourself. Assure the Countess there is nothing to worry about and that we shall be back this evening with a fine hare for supper.'

'What is this all about?' Alexis demanded, as he followed the priest away from the other men and along a narrow path that wound deep into the forest. 'I do not like leaving Natalia alone. There is something happening which I do not understand and do not like.'

The priest sighed.

'I am to blame. For many years I have cared for these people and thought I knew and understood them. But now I, with all my book learning and experience, have been unable – so they tell me – to drive out the evil spirits that have killed their cattle and goats and will attack their sheep and finally the peasants themselves. Tonight the women will seek to succeed where I have failed.'

'The women? How?'

'All I can tell you is what I have gathered from the men when they have drunk too much. No man has ever seen the procession or the ritual, yet they know that tonight the women intend to plough a furrow all round the village without yoking any animal. They believe this furrow will allow the good spirits to come out of the earth and destroy the evil ones which have brought sickness and death.

'It is obvious that this is some ancient pagan rite, but what else may be done, none of the men appears to know. It has never been enacted while I have lived here but I have just been told that no man has any authority until the ceremony is over and that tonight every man must remain indoors no matter what

63

sounds he may hear. They say the women would tear limb from limb any man who dared to spy on them.'

Alexis, who had listened incredulously at first, made up his mind quickly, knowing that now was no time to talk of the phantom girl, the hidden skull and the bridal gown.

'Father Peter. I believe Natalia and I are in danger. It is possible the peasants blame Natalia for this sickness because she was feverish when we came here. I beg of you to lend me your horse so that we can go away without delay.'

'It is too late, Count Alexis. The peasants would not let you leave. But I promise that I personally will see that neither of you comes to any harm.

'When we return to the village we must go straight to the Widow Anna's cottage and stay with the Countess. When the ceremony is over all the women, including the Widow Anna, will return exhausted to sleep in the big barn: the men will have drunk themselves insensible during this time. As soon as it is safe we shall saddle your horse and the Countess shall have mine.

'Take this path we have followed today through the forest. Rather less than a mile from here a very narrow, overgrown track on the right leads down to the river where there is a ford. Ride straight on to the west and in four hours you will reach the estate of a good friend of mine. Tell him I sent you. He will arrange for you to travel safely by coach to Moscow.'

He broke off as one of the men hurried up to them and began to talk excitedly, pointing back to the village. The priest frowned, asked an abrupt question and nodded his head.

'There has been an accident in a nearby hamlet,

Count Alexis. I must go at once. Come back with me to the village and go straight to your Countess. Rest assured I shall be back in time to send you on your way.'

The village square was deserted except for one old woman who was keeping an eye on the priest's horse which had been saddled and was waiting for him.

'Go to your Countess now,' he said, as he swung himself into the saddle. 'All will be well.'

For a moment Alexis watched him ride off and then he turned and hurried to the Widow Anna's cottage, noticing now that whereas all the other cottage doors and windows were open, only the Widow's door was closed, the window shuttered.

'Natalia!' he called out, flinging open the door, but after the brightness of the sunshine he could see nothing. 'Natalia!' No one moved or spoke. There was no fire burning in the hearth.

Suddenly someone pushed him violently into the room and the door was slammed shut.

Angry and frightened he picked himself up and groped about in the darkness. Natalia's bed was there but not Natalia. There was no sign of the Widow Anna. Stumbling over stools and overturning the table, he made his way back to the door, banging on it with clenched fists.

'Let me out! Let me out at once!'

There was no sound outside.

A terrible fear gripped him and returning to the fireplace he groped along the central beam above his head.

The cloth bundle with its sheep's skull and white bridal dress was no longer there. What ancient sorcery and evil were about to be practised?

This hut is only made of wood, he thought, fighting against the panic which threatened to overwhelm him, for he dared not think in what danger Natalia now stood among these fear-crazed peasants. There must be some spade or shovel, some tool to help him force open the door. Perhaps in one of the cupboards . . .?

But even as he felt his way to the wall he was conscious of a change in the atmosphere and he sensed that he was no longer alone.

'Who is that?' he asked sharply. 'Where are you?' And he swung his arms about in an effort to find who was there.

'Please sit down and listen to me,' a soft voice entreated. 'If you wait I will help you when the time comes.'

'Who are you? How can you expect me to wait when my betrothed is in danger?'

'Trust me. Please trust me. There is nothing you can do now but wait. I must leave you for the time being but I promise you will save your lovely Countess. Rest now, for later you will need all your strength.'

'Wait. Do not go yet. Tell me who you are and why you are here.'

He heard a soft, heart-breaking sigh.

'Once I was a bride – oh, so long ago. But the women said the Earth Spirits needed me.'

'Was it you Natalia saw here last night?'

'Yes. I tried to warn her but I had almost forgotten how to speak. And I wanted to ask her to help me for I am so weary, so tired of wandering alone, unseen, unloved, throughout the long, long years.

'If you will trust me I will return when the time

66

comes and your bride will be safe. Trust me. Please trust me. And rest.'

Now he knew he was alone again.

Half-crazed with doubt and fear, he stumbled across to Natalia's bed and threw himself on it.

Trust a phantom bride? Believe the word of a ghost?

He ought to be deciding how to rescue Natalia but a voice inside kept on telling him to rest even though this was the last thing he wanted to do.

His eyes closed.

He did not hear the men returning to the village, shouting and laughing. He did not hear the other cottage doors being shut and the windows darkened, or know that inside the men drank their fermented liquor until they were insensible so that there was no injury to their pride while for a few hours that night it was their women who ruled.

Alexis woke as the door creaked slowly open. Above the cluster of cottages opposite he could see a sky full of stars.

And then she came in, an ethereal light illuminating the pale composed face of the phantom bride, the wild flowers in the dark hair, the white gown with its sinister stain. But when he saw the dagger in her right hand he drew back in horror.

'Have no fear, Count Alexis,' she said softly.

'They – sacrificed you?' he asked dully and then he sprang to his feet. 'Those mad old peasant women mean to sacrifice my bride too.'

'Be calm, Count Alexis. With your help what once happened out there will never happen again. I promise you that your Countess will be safe if only you will be guided by me.'

Suddenly the silence was shattered by a fearful howling and shrieking, a shrill and piercing yelling that rose and fell and rose again.

'Wild animals!' he cried.

'Not animals. Women,' the soft voice said sadly. 'They are maddened, frenzied with the power they know they possess tonight. You must wait until the furrow is almost complete and their force spent so that they cannot give chase.'

Louder and hoarser, more and more frenetic grew the screaming and now between the wooden church and the first cluster of cottages he saw the fearful procession led by the Widow Anna, dressed in a white shift and with her head covered by a shawl, hitched to a plough driven by two other old women. Behind them came others, their grey hair blowing about their faces, brandishing scythes and waving lanterns as they threw back their heads and rent the night air with strident shouting.

'No, the beautiful Countess is not among those,' the phantom bride assured Alexis as his eyes passed from one ugly distorted face to another.

A second group of women followed, carrying animal skulls on the end of long poles, screeching and sobbing and moaning in a wild abandoned frenzy that now bordered on madness.

'Wait, Please wait. She is safe at present,' the soft voice implored as the stars and the jerking lanterns revealed the last figure, swaying, stumbling in her white bridal dress, a garland of wild flowers in her long dark hair, a dagger clutched in her right hand. 'They can do nothing until the Widow Anna has ploughed the furrow round the village and the circle is completed where it began – beyond the church.

'But tonight the circle will not be completed. Together we shall prevent it. You will save your Countess and I – at last – shall be able to rest. So please trust me. And wait.'

'How long must I wait?'

'About two hours.'

To wait two hours, watching these demented women stumbling, falling, rising again as they appeared and disappeared between the groups of cottages: to listen for two hours to that harsh shouting, that horrible clamour, watching as the Widow Anna staggered under the burden of the plough and at the rear of the dreadful procession Natalia walked like one in a trance ... it was more than Alexis could bear.

'Wait,' the soft voice begged. 'Trust me. Wait.'

Shrill and coarse and agonised rose the screams as the women invoked their old pagan gods, and somehow Alexis heeded that soft voice although each minute seemed like an hour. And then, at last, the phantom bride tightened her grasp on her dagger and whispered, 'Now!'

'What must I do?' Alexis asked, knowing he could trust her completely.

'Keep in the shadows and go to the stable where your horse is saddled and awaits you. The Widow Anna has almost completed her furrow. Ride straight towards your Countess but keep an eye on the dagger she holds for she has been given drugs and is mindlessly obeying the Widow's orders, even as I did. Go now.'

It took him less than a minute to reach the stable, lead out his horse and mount, and then leaning forward he urged it on, his eyes fixed on that last swaying, silent figure.

Suddenly the wild hysterical shrieks of the women changed and there was fear and panic in their cries. No one turned as his horse thundered up to Natalia, no one saw him seize her and swing her up in front of him or strike from her hand the dagger which she aimed at her heart.

Away to the forest track he galloped, aware that a dreadful silence had fallen on that terrifying procession.

'She is there,' Natalia murmured, her words slurred as she tried to shake off the effects of the herbal infusion she had been forced to drink and which had deprived her of will power. 'My little phantom bride stands facing the Widow Anna so that she cannot complete the circle. They can all see her now, a garland of wild flowers in her hair, blood staining her bridal gown and dripping from the dagger she holds so high.

'How terrified they are! The women killed her long ago when the furrow was complete. They had no wish to murder but the Earth Spirits demanded a life.'

Alexis glanced back briefly.

The women might have been carved from stone. And then one by one they collapsed and lay moaning and twitching on the ground. Only the phantom bride stood erect. Across her face passed a look of gratitude and great tranquillity: the dagger dropped from her hand and she disappeared. Whoever she was and whenever it was she had lived – and died – at last she would rest in peace.

6   Terror in the Tatras

On the outskirts of a village in the foothills of the
Tatra Mountains in Poland there once dwelt a forester
and his wife, with two children, a girl and a boy,
whom they loved dearly.

When summer came the children played in front of
the two-roomed wooden cottage the forester himself
had built, and his wife spun and wove and sewed,
while her husband worked in the pine forests that
stretched up the great mountain ranges to the east
and to the north.

But all too soon the winter was on them, when the
days were dark, the winds bitter and the snow came
whirling down, covering cottages and ground and
trees.

First the pond and then the river froze, and as it
grew steadily colder and colder and the snow continued to fall, from high up in the forests came the
first howls of foraging wolf packs. Then all the work
out of doors had to be done in the short hours of
daylight, and the forester and other men of the village
were careful never to venture far into the forest alone,
and they always returned home before nightfall and
saw all doors were barred, all windows firmly closed.

As the cold increased, the howls of the hungry
wolves grew louder as they searched for food, for an

71

unwary hare or fox, for a reindeer weakened by injury or a bear grown too old to defend itself; but sometimes, when the hunt had been unsuccessful and the villagers looked out of their windows in the pale light of the early morning, they saw the dreaded prints in the fallen snow and they hurried out to make sure their pigs and geese and ducks and hens were safe in the outhouses and cellars.

Each year the long cruel winter claimed its victims, generally from among the very old or the very young.

It was early one spring, when the girl was nine and her brother seven, that their mother took to her bed and died.

'What is to become of us now?' the forester asked despairingly when they returned to the cottage after the funeral.

'I have already put some of our bread and goats' milk cheese in your bag,' the little girl said. 'Take your axe and go into the forest and work as you have always done. My brother and I will look after you and our home and all our stock.'

Shaking his head doubtfully, the forester did as he was bid. Heavy-hearted he worked in the forest and heavy-hearted he returned home, but the minute he opened the door and saw the floor swept, the beds made and the dumplings bobbing about in the soup in the iron cauldron above the fire, he gathered the children in his arms and wept for the last time.

'I shall miss your mother for the rest of my life,' he said, 'but together we shall look after one another.'

'Will the pain inside of me always hurt?' the little boy asked that night.

'It will grow less until you scarcely feel it,' his sister

72

assured him, and she hoped that this would indeed be so.

As the summer months passed the children still missed their mother, but because they worked so hard in the cottage and in the common fields which belonged to everyone in the village, their grief, although they did not realize it, was not quite as sharp as it had been.

They prepared for the winter exactly as their mother had done, drying herbs and plants, berries and mushrooms and fungi, and salting their share of the birds and beasts for which the villagers had decided there would not be enough food and so had slaughtered and divided amongst the households.

The last carp were caught in the village pond, the last trout in the river before they were frozen over, and once again the bitter winds blew down from the north bringing with them the swirling snowflakes, and it was not long before the hungry wolves ventured nearer and nearer the village by night in search of something – anything – to eat.

One evening the forester returned late from a meeting the priest had called to arrange for a fatherless family to be cared for: the children were asleep on their straw mattresses in front of the kitchen fire and, pausing only to adjust the woven blankets and the sheepskins which covered them, he went quietly to his lonely bed in the other room and quickly fell asleep.

Presently he stirred uneasily and then sat up, wondering why it was so light and then realizing that although he had double-barred the door, he had forgotten to close the shutters of his little window, and the moon had risen and was peering in with its pale, unearthly light.

Drawing about him the fur pelts which his wife had sewn together as their bed covering, he stared, fascinated by the dazzling circle of light, wondering why he had never before noticed how big and splendid and at the same time how frightening the moon was. He leaned forward to look more closely, but suddenly the rays were cut off as the head of an animal covered with white fur and with deep-set eyes appeared at the window, and first one paw was raised and then a second as though in entreaty. When the animal saw that it held his attention it threw back its head so that the moonlight caught its strange dark eyes as it howled, mournfully but very softly.

'A wolf!' he cried in horror. He leaped out of bed, pulled on his clothes and boots, and seizing his lantern and gun walked quickly and quietly through the kitchen. But as he drew back the second of the heavy wooden bars which held the door securely closed, his daughter stirred.

'What is it, Father?' she asked sleepily.

'A wolf. A great white wolf. I mean to go out and shoot it. Bar the door after me, child.'

'Oh, Father, it is not safe for you to go out alone at night,' the little girl cried, but the snowflakes swirling in the moonlight dazzled her, and though she could hear her father shouting at the creature and caught occasional glimpses of his lantern as he entered the forest, it seemed to her that all the world outside was filled with the eerie howling of the wolf, and as it grew fainter and fainter she thought she could distinguish a mocking note such as she had never heard before in the cry of any wild animal.

Troubled, she barred the door, hesitated and then

opened the shutters of the kitchen window so that the firelight might shine out, and returned to her bed.

And waited.

Farther and farther into the woods the forester plunged where frozen snow weighed down the branches of the pine trees: on and on he forced his way following the tracks of the great white wolf until the moonlight no longer penetrated the snow-shrouded canopy of interlocking branches and he was completely dependent on his lantern.

What a magnificent creature it was. And white! It was the first time he had ever seen a white wolf. He was determined the creature should fall to his gun and was filled with a wild exultation at the thought. Obviously the creature must be the leader of the pack.

The pack?

He halted.

What had come over him? It was madness for him to hunt for a wolf by night, madness to leave his children alone and unprotected.

Hastily he turned, and just as he started to retrace his steps he heard a terrified cry.

'Help! Help! Oh, help me!'

'Who is it?' he shouted. 'Where are you?'

'I am here. Close by. Oh, help me.'

Holding up his lantern, he saw a fur-clad figure stumbling through the trees towards him.

'The wolves – the wolves have followed me all night and will not let me be. Oh, save me, forester, please save me for I am all alone now and fear I can struggle no farther.'

Startled, the forester looked down at the weeping woman and then stared around him, listening intently. Had he frightened away that white wolf and its pack?

'Come with me, lady,' he said gruffly, 'the sooner we are out of the forest the better.' And taking her arm he hurried back following his own track, half dragging, half supporting her to where the firelight shone like a beacon through the kitchen window.

'Let me in, children,' he called out as he approached the door. 'I have a traveller with me who has just escaped from wolves.'

He heard the heavy wooden bars being drawn, and at last they were safe inside the warm kitchen.

With a sigh of exhaustion the traveller sank in front of the fire, pulled off first her fur mittens and then her fur hat, and her hair fell to her waist in a cascade of palest gold.

As she shrugged herself free of her fur coat, the little boy, awakened by the arrival, sat up and stared at the woman in her richly embroidered dress, and reaching out a hand, touched the pale gold hair.

'Are you a princess?' he asked, and now he touched the velvet gown.

The lady smiled and held out her arms, and as the boy hesitated she leaned forward, lifted him on to her lap and kissed him lightly on the brow.

'These are your children?' she asked, turning to the forester. 'They are adorable.' And she stretched out an arm to the daughter, but the little girl shrank away, busying herself with the fire and pretending not to notice.

'Are you a princess?' the little boy repeated, and the lady shook her head and smiled sadly.

'There is a bed for you in the second room,' the

forester said. 'I shall sleep here on the floor with the children. You will be safe with us.'

'I am not tired yet,' the lady said. 'Let me stay here a while by the fire and watch the children sleep and do you keep me company.'

The boy fell asleep at once but the girl was troubled and though she closed her eyes, sleep would not come. Soon she heard her father speak to the lady.

'Tomorrow you must let me know what I can do to help you, for though you say you are not a princess, I know you must be a great lady and I think you have never before been inside a cottage as humble as this.'

'I am a lady and my father is rich, but in his castle I have never known such kindness as surrounds me here.

'My father wished me to marry a friend of his, an old man whom I feared and disliked. When he would not listen to my pleading, I offered my groom money and jewels if he would help me to escape and drive me to relations who are more understanding than my parents.

'He readily agreed. We set off last night but in the snowstorm we lost our way. It was not long before a pack of wolves picked up our scent and began to follow us, knowing that soon the horses must tire. When one stumbled, my groom bade me jump and flee while he fought off the pack. Even as I protested the leading horse fell and the sledge with all my possessions and jewels overturned and I was thrown to one side. My head struck against a tree and I lost consciousness.

'When I recovered I was alone. Somehow the groom must have driven on, but far away I could hear

the long drawn-out howling of the wolves and I knew
. . . I knew . . .' She shivered. 'To you I owe my life.'

'Go to your bed now and sleep,' the forester said.
'There is nothing I or anyone can do tonight. But
know that you can remain under my roof as long as
you wish, and know that here you will always be safe.'

That night the little girl was awake long after
everyone else was asleep, for she was filled with a fear
she could not understand.

The next morning the forester set out for the place
in the forest where he had encountered the lady,
intent on tracing her sledge and discovering the fate
of her groom and horses. So heavily had the snow
fallen it had almost obliterated the tracks they had
made the previous night but at last he reached a small
clearing where the snow was churned and bore the
deep prints of wolves and men: fresh snow flakes were
settling on ugly brown stains which had recently been
red.

'What the wolves did not devour, robbers have
stolen,' he said when he returned.

On hearing this, the lady wept bitterly.

'Alas! Now I have neither the means nor the money
to continue my journey,' she lamented. 'What is to
become of me?'

'Stay with us until summer comes, and then whatever you want to do, I shall help you,' the forester
said, whereupon the little boy hugged her, but the
little girl turned away, wondering why the lady had
no thoughts for the groom who had saved her life at
the expense of his own.

During the day the lady saw to the meals and the
care of the cottage and played with the children, and
the little boy loved her, but the little girl feared her

and watched silently when her father came home and the lady waited on him and sat at his feet and listened to him as he talked about his work and the people in the village in a way he had never talked to her or her brother.

With the coming of spring and the melting of the snow and ice the lady wept again

'I have been so happy here,' she said, 'and now I must leave you and I do not want to do that, for you three are dearer to me than my own relations.'

'Then stay with us always,' the forester begged. 'Be my wife and the mother of my dear children.' And the little girl saw that so infatuated was her father that in less than a year he had forgotten all about their real mother, and she feared the lady more than ever.

The next day the forester and the lady went down into the village to visit the priest and to ask him to marry them, but there they found the old man had been taken ill very suddenly. However, another priest who happened to be passing, agreed to marry them there and then before continuing on his journey.

Delighted with his beautiful lady wife the forester returned to his cottage, and though the little boy was nearly as happy as his father, the little girl was uneasy and afraid.

And with good reason. For now she was safely married, the lady sent the children to work in the fields all the time their father was away from home, and only when he returned did she make a pretence of speaking to them kindly.

'Let us tell our father how cruel she is to us,' the boy whispered to his sister one day, for they had been sent out to work without anything to eat.

'Not yet. Have patience,' his sister advised, and she

gave him a stale crust that their stepmother had thrown out for the pig.

One night not long afterwards, when the moon hung full in the sky, some sound awakened the girl, and she saw her stepmother, barefooted and clothed only in a long white nightgown, open the door, and then through the window she watched her run from the cottage and down the silent village street.

Trembling, she lay down again and waited and just before daybreak she saw her stepmother return, her hands and nightgown stained and red with what could only be blood. Horrified she watched as the lady took off the nightgown, placed it on the fire and watched it burn: after that she washed her hands, threw the water away and then crept into the bed where her husband, the forester, slept so soundly.

A month later, when the moon was again full, the stepmother once more slipped out of the cottage, but this time the girl followed her, for she remembered something she had heard in the village the previous day – how a young girl had unexpectedly died to the sorrow of her family, and she remembered too how four weeks before another young girl had died, the first such death for many months.

Keeping in the dark shadows, the girl hurried down the silent street; but just as the stepmother reached the churchyard a cloud hid the moon and when the first beam shone down again, the lady had vanished and in her place stood a huge white wolf.

For a moment the creature stood motionless, sniffing the air, and then it bounded over the low wall and ran towards a recently filled grave and began to dig with its forepaws.

Terrified, the girl turned and ran back home and lay shivering in bed. She was still awake although she pretended to sleep when her stepmother returned just before daybreak, and again she watched as the lady burned her bloodstained nightgown and washed her hands.

When she told her brother what she had seen, he laughed.

'That was a bad dream,' he said, as they worked together in the fields. 'How could our new mother have burned her nightgown when she has only one and I can see it now hanging on the washing line?'

The girl stood up and looked across at the garment and could not understand how this was so.

'Watch with me the next time after someone in the village has died and the moon is full,' she begged.

'I will try to stay awake,' he promised. 'But I work so hard during the day that I fall asleep as soon as I crawl into bed. Waken me when the time comes.'

Anxiously the girl waited for news from the village and she sighed with relief when she knew that no one was ill and no one had died. This night I shall be able to sleep, she thought, taking a last look at the full moon, but soon a familiar sound wakened her and she saw her stepmother slipping out of the door for the third time.

'Wake up! Wake up!' she urged, tugging at her brother's arm, but he slept on for all the world as though he were drugged.

And so she set off alone, keeping to the dark shadows of the silent street until she saw her stepmother stop outside the churchyard.

This time no cloud covered the moon.

This time she saw her stepmother tear off her nightgown and immediately change into a great white wolf, and she screamed out in fear and shrank back against the wall as the terrible creature leaped on her.

Awakened by that cry the church verger flung open his window and leaned out.

'A wolf!' he shouted. 'A great white wolf attacking a child!' And he discharged the gun he always kept ready to hand, whereupon the wolf dropped the girl, seized the nightgown between its teeth and bounded away through the village.

'It is the forester's daughter and she must have been sleepwalking when the wolf attacked her,' the verger's wife said. 'How are we to tell her father?'

They carried the dead girl into their cottage, washed those savage bites and dressed her in white, and they placed a single wild white flower in her clasped hands.

The following day the girl was buried and the stepmother sobbed louder than anyone, louder even than the forester, but in the boy's eyes there was suspicion as well as grief.

Seven days later he went to the forge opposite the church, where the smith was busy at work.

'I have come to you for advice,' he said, 'for you are the wisest man in the village. All evil things fear you because of your power over cold and hot iron.'

'What advice canI give you?' the smith asked.

'Two nights ago I had a dream,' the boy said. 'I dreamed that the moon was full and my sister went out and a big white werewolf attacked her and killed her. I woke and was afraid.

'Last night I dreamed again. Once more there was

a full moon and the white werewolf went hungry to the churchyard to dig up my sister and devour her.'

'Have you told your father?' the smith asked.

'He would not believe me.'

'Or the priest?'

'He is old and ill and would not understand.'

'For a long time I have known there was evil in the village,' the smith said slowly, 'but until now I did not know how great that evil was. You did well to come to me for counsel.

'Return to your home and behave as though your grief was for a sister killed by accident. When next the moon is full, go to the forest where your father is working and ask him to come here with you as we are holding a solemn service in honour of his daughter. Do not let him return to his cottage.'

'And you will protect my sister?'

'I give you my word that your sister, and indeed many others, will be protected.'

From every man who stopped at the forge the smith asked a silver coin, a silver button or a piece of a silver buckle or brooch, and everyone knew the reason and gave willingly: these tokens the smith melted down and made into a silver bullet.

The women, knowing what was afoot and aware of the peril in which they all stood, brought to the forge what bread and spirits they could spare.

On the night of the next full moon all the men gathered in the forge and there the forester and his son joined them. Silently they ate and drank. Silently they waited.

It was nearly two hours later that they saw her

running down the street, her pale gold hair blowing in the wind, now covering and now revealing her lovely face, and so lightly did she move that her bare feet scarcely seemed to touch the ground.

The forester would have hurried out to her but the others held him back.

'Wait,' they murmured. 'Wait and watch.'

She had reached the churchyard now and there she stopped, tore off her nightgown and the next moment in her place stood a huge white wolf: lifting its head it sniffed the air and then it bounded over the low wall, making for the place where the girl had been buried twenty-seven days previously.

'Now?' the men asked quietly.

'Now,' the smith agreed, and lifting his gun to his shoulder, he took careful aim and fired, and the silver bullet penetrated the white fur and lodged in the creature's heart.

Lifting up its head for the last time, the werewolf gave one long agonised howl and then collapsed. It was dead by the time the men reached it.

'I suspected nothing of this,' the forester said. 'I thought her beautiful and unfortunate. I took her into my home in her need, but she brought only evil and terror and death with her.'

He helped the men bury the werewolf at a lonely place far from the village and when they had set a huge stone over the grave, he took his son by the hand, and together they set off for a new life in some far-off village where no one would know of the cruel white werewolf and the evil it had brought to innocent people.

7 The Cromarty Vow

'If I stay at this lykewake any longer I shall weep,' Christie whispered to her friend, Jeannie, 'and that would prevent the soul leaving the dead child's body.'

Both girls looked apprehensively from the still figure on the bed to the village women now gathered round the fire, laughing and drinking and joking. The three empty dishes which the girls had set so carefully on the hearth had been kicked to one side and most of the three handfuls of salt had been spilled from the bowl placed on the shrouded body.

'Let us go,' Christie urged. 'All we came to do has been undone. This is now no place for you or me.'

Silently they stole from the room, leaving the door wide open, but before they reached the barn where ever since they had been children they had met and exchanged confidences, they heard the farm door being slammed shut.

'All the windows are closed too,' Jeannie said, looking back in dismay. 'How will her poor soul escape?' And they both thought of the little flame-soul searching hopelessly for the three empty dishes which signified faith and hope and courage, and then battering itself against the closed doors and windows in its attempt to get out.

'And if it does escape, how will it pay its way on

the journey to the next world?' the elder girl asked. 'With my own eyes I saw the henwife steal the penny I put in the cold hand of the little orphan. Steal from a corpse! How could anyone be so wicked?'

'And when one of the women choked and coughed and blew out the saining candle, that has been blessed and must burn continuously to keep away all evil spirits, they just laughed and took their time in lighting it again.'

'It must be the saddest thing in the world to be an orphan. No one cared about her when she was alive – except us. No one cares about her when she is dead – except us. But the village women do not listen to us because we are young.'

They sat amongst the hay, listening to the muted laughter and shouts from those who attended the lykewake – the customary watch that was always kept from the time someone died until they were buried. They remembered the careless way in which the body had been washed and laid out, how roughly it had been dressed in its torn shroud.

No looking-glass had been covered, no clock stopped.

It was only a little orphan servant girl who had died, and no one at the lykewake cared whether her body rested in peace in the earth or what happened to her frightened questing soul.

'It will not be like this when it is our turn to die,' Jeannie said. 'We have mothers who will see our bodies are washed and shriven and dressed in linen: we have fathers who will make sure that saining candles burn all the time at the head and foot of our coffins; and we have brothers and sisters who will watch day and night and pray for us until we are buried, and they will do everything to help our souls on their long journey to peace and happiness.'

'We have mothers and fathers now,' said Christie – who was older than Jeannie by two years. 'But fathers and mothers die before their children. And as for our brothers and sisters, who knows where they will be when it is our turn to die? Already two of my brothers have left Scotland for a new life in Australia, and though they promised faithfully to write, we know neither where they are nor what has become of them.'

The girls looked at each other, seeking some form of solace for the future.

'We have been close friends ever since we were little children,' Christie said at last. 'Let us each make a solemn vow and promise that whoever dies first, the other will go at once and lay out the body and see that all is done according to the old customs and traditions throughout the lykewake, so that the body may rest and the soul depart to the next world without hindrance.'

'Yes,' Jeannie agreed eagerly. 'Let us make that vow now and remember it until the time comes when one of us must keep it.'

The years passed.

In that remote village in Cromarty, in the far north of Scotland the two girls grew up, were courted and married, and went away, each with her own husband to live on farms distant from the village and from each other. Now their lives were centred on the work of their farms, on caring for their husbands and those who worked for them.

So busy were they that they met only rarely and by

chance at some market or fair, where they exchanged a few words and smiled before parting.

Jeannie, now mistress of a farm on the hill of Nigg, had just fed her bairn and placed it, warmly wrapped, in the sweet-smelling straw in its cradle when a shepherd who lived higher up the hill rode past her kitchen window and reined his horse at her open back door.

'I have no time to stop now, mistress,' he called out as she hurried across the kitchen to greet him. 'I have business to attend to and am on my way to the fair. But I thought it right to tell you the sad news of one I know to have been an old friend of yours before she married and went to live in Fearn. I fear it will grieve you much, but I have just heard that Christie died last night in childbed – and her bairn too.'

Jeannie, her heart filled with sorrow for the loss of her friend, could not help weeping, but it was not until the shepherd had ridden off that she remembered the vow she had made so long ago.

What can I do to keep my promise, she thought anxiously.

She was alone on the farm with her bairn, for her husband, the ploughman and the maid had all left early that morning for the fair and would not be back until late in the evening.

I promised Christie I would lay out her body without delay, she thought, and see that all is done according to the old customs and traditions throughout the lykewake, but now I cannot leave the farm and the beasts unattended. How can I fulfil my vow?

As the hours passed she became more and more desperate.

At first she comforted herself with the hope that someone at the fair would tell her husband about the death of her childhood friend, and he would return home earlier than usual. But that comfort soon fled as she remembered her husband knew nothing of her promise and so would have no reason for curtailing his rare day away from the hard work of the farm.

Unhappy and ill at ease she occupied herself with the maid's work and her own household duties, fed her bairn, saw to the farm affairs and then, towards evening, brought the cows into their shed, which was built onto the side of the house. She tied the beasts in their stalls and though she talked to them soothingly and hummed as she milked them, she did not gain her usual pleasure and satisfaction from her work.

After that she fed the bairn again, returned him to his cradle beside the fire and then shut up the hens, for only the previous night her husband had glimpsed a fox prowling round the farm.

She walked slowly back into the kitchen but, the feeling of unease mounting remorselessly, at last she drew her shawl over her head and shoulders and went out into the gathering darkness.

She climbed up a grassy hillock which overlooked the moor and her eyes searched the track winding among the coarse grass and heather and bracken to their farmhouse.

To her relief it was not long before she saw the figure of a woman dressed in white moving swiftly along the track towards her. The maid at last, she thought, and she hurried back to the house because she did not want the girl to think she was waiting for her, grudging her a few hours of pleasure with her friends away from the labour and lonely life of the farm.

As she passed the open doors of the cowshed, the cattle suddenly began to stamp and snort and pull at their tethers as though something – or someone – had frightened them. Turning and looking back to see what this might be, she was gripped by a terrible fear – it was not her maid who was gliding so quickly towards her but a tall form in a winding sheet!

Trembling, she ran into the kitchen, snatched the bairn from his cradle and hugging him to her, sat down close to the fire and, eyes wide with guilt and fear, she watched the figure come in through the door, cross the room and sit on the farmer's chair on the opposite side of the fireplace.

Slowly the figure raised thin pale arms up to its head, slowly the fingers fumbled at the winding sheet, tugging and pulling until its face was revealed and the mistress of the farm found herself looking at the countenance of Christie, her childhood friend.

Fearfully she shrank back, holding the bairn ever closer to her, for in those glassy eyes that stared at her from the white face there was a wild and bitter anger.

In vain she tried to explain why she had been unable to keep her promise, but terror had left her dumb: in vain she tried to look away, but those glaring eyes held hers and the anger in them seemed to be a vital, threatening force in that dead body.

And so they sat, the living woman and the angry dead, neither speaking, neither moving.

Lower and lower burned the fire, and as the shadows took over the room Jeannie knew she could not move from where she sat and must stay alone with the phantom in the increasing darkness. And when all the light was gone then, she knew, she would be in the power of the angry dead.

As the last lingering flames began to die down in the fireplace Jeannie, her eyes still on the other's, stretched out one hand, slowly, cautiously to her bairn's cradle, grasped a little of the straw there and threw it on the fire, and the little flames that sprang up gave light and comforted her.

Again and again she replenished the fire with straw until her groping fingers scraped along the bottom of the cradle and came up with the very last fragments.

There was nothing now to save her, she thought, as she flung them on the dying fire – but then she heard the clatter of horses' hooves and laughter and cheerful voices outside.

At the same moment the phantom rose silently and glided out of the door. As it passed the cowshed, again the cattle stamped and snorted as though frightened, and the cow in the last stall kicked out with its hind leg, and it seemed to Jeannie, watching by the fire, that the white figure cried out in pain, seemed to stumble and then suddenly disappeared.

The maid came into the kitchen just in time to save the bairn as her mistress fell to the floor in a faint.

Early the next morning, her senses restored thanks to the care of her husband and maid, but still distraught and sad, Jeannie rode off to the farm where her friend had lived, for her husband agreed that late though it was, she must keep her promise to attend the lykewake and see that all was done according to the old customs and traditions.

'I am grateful that you have come,' the mourning farmer said when she had told him of her vow. 'Last night I tossed and turned in despair, knowing there was something which had to be done here but not knowing what it was. Now I am convinced that my poor young wife would never have rested had you not come to keep your promise.'

He took her into the room where Christie lay, with the stillborn bairn by her side.

And first Jeannie opened all the doors and windows; and then she shrouded the looking-glass so that the souls of mother and bairn should not be confused by their own reflection: after that she stopped all the clocks, for the dead have nothing to do with time. By the fire she placed three empty dishes and on a side table set two bowls each containing three handfuls of salt, which signified life eternal.

Now she attended to the laying out of the bodies of the dead.

First she washed and blessed and dressed the bairn and placed a coin in its tiny hand; and then, with gentle and loving care she washed and tended Christie, remembering the days of their childhood together.

But not all the washing in the world, no matter how hard she tried, could remove a strange mark – as though made by a blow from a hoof – plain to be seen below the knee of her dead friend.

8   The Transylvanian Horror

My name is Christian Rheinhard. I am eighteen years of age and a cornet in the First Regiment of Hussars of the Emperor Franz Josef – a regiment famous throughout Europe for its valour in the field and its splendour on the parade ground.

I have no experience of writing, except of army reports and letters to my parents and relatives in Melk and Linz, but so horrifying have been the events of the last few days that I have determined to set them down on paper while they are fresh in my mind.

The Colonel of my troop comes of a wealthy aristocratic Viennese family with a distinguished military tradition: the Captain and Lieutenant both bear famous Austrian names, as indeed I do myself.

Life was extremely pleasant for us when we were at our headquarters in Vienna. We rode, fenced, boxed and exercised in the gymnasium and kept ourselves in perfect physical condition.

For our frequent parades, the grooms saw to our horses, their saddles and harness, and the valets to our uniforms, spurs, swords and pistols, so that when we rode through the streets of Vienna the people crowded on to the narrow pavements and cheered at the splendour of our appearance.

Naturally when we were off duty we were in great

demand at court and in the old palaces and great houses of the aristocracy. However, my Colonel, an old friend of the family, considered I was too young for society life with all its pleasures and temptations. I suspect my mother had something to do with this, for I had been very strictly brought up on our estate on the banks of the Danube – and I was put under the care of a tutor who required me to spend a great deal of my time studying in my rooms.

As I was shy and of a serious turn of mind and found much pleasure in my books, this confinement to my quarters did not worry me and so perhaps I was the only one who had no regrets when, without warning, we were told the troop had been posted to some place with an unpronounceable name in Transylvania. It appeared that there was the threat of trouble among certain landowners and their peasants, who did not approve of their country being merged with our great Austro-Hungarian Empire.

Three days later, after a flurry of last-minute arrangements and much weeping on the part of wives and sweethearts we rode out of Vienna and, leaving Austria and all we held dear behind, began the crossing of the great Hungarian plain. Fertile the land might have been, but we were not impressed by the sight of the occasional peasant toiling in the sun and here and there a miserable hut thatched with turf, and it seemed to me that all I had heard about the backwardness and poverty of these Hungarians was only too true and that they were still living in the Dark Ages.

There was little to cheer us up when we reached the Carpathian Mountains of Transylvania and rode up a gloomy valley, following the course of a river hemmed in on both sides by steep, thickly-wooded slopes, the foothills of the towering mountain range beyond. At last the valley opened out, the ground underfoot became soft and marshy and when we set eyes on the long, low wooden building with its stables and outbuildings at the foot of a rocky crag, our hearts sank.

In Vienna we had been told that although it was many years since the station had been occupied, local peasant women had been given orders to clean and prepare the barracks for us, but the moment we dismounted and entered the front door we were filled with anger and dismay, for it was obvious that whatever orders had been given, none had been carried out.

That night we had to water, feed and groom our own horses before we sat down to cold meats: fortunately we had brought plenty of wine in which to drown our unhappiness and discontent.

Next day the Colonel rode off to the nearest town to storm over the laziness of those who had forgotten to prepare and victual the barracks, and then, meeting only indifference among officials, he made his own arrangements for our men to collect supplies there regularly, as he meant to keep the same high standard in the mess as in Vienna.

We were instructed to patrol the valley and the foothills around us with a view to establishing good relations with local landowners, farmers and peasants and we were to find out how serious were the threats of an uprising: in this we were singularly unsuccessful, as though we were all fluent in our native German, and in French and Italian, the district was sparsely populated and such local people as we met could not understand us or we them, so outlandish was their own tongue.

It was a dull life after Vienna, and the summer heat trapped in that valley was oppressive, but we accustomed ourselves to it, as soldiers must.

One evening, when I was off duty, I took my fishing rod to a spot upstream that I thought might offer some shade, if not a catch, and I was just preparing my bait when someone coughed behind me. I looked up to see a personable youth in plain but clean peasant clothes: dark, curling hair framed an oval face and his dark eyes looked thoughtful and intelligent.

'If you are interested in a fine pike, Herr Cornet, there is one at rest just a little farther upstream by those bushes.'

His German was excellent, and as the place he indicated was within range of our sentries, I followed him, cast my line and within a few minutes had landed a splendid fish. His pleasure was almost equal to mine as I continued to increase my catch, and in answer to my questions, he explained that he was a harbourer, his work being to care for the deer of his master the Count, who lived some distance away in the Carpathians and who owned most of the forests around us.

Naturally I informed my Colonel of my meeting with Stefan – for such was his name – and he agreed that the youth might indeed prove useful to the troop later if he could obtain permission for us to hunt over the Count's lands and also act as a guide and interpreter. Life, he thought, would be much less tedious for us all if this could be secured.

The following day Stefan was waiting for me by the river and asked me if I would be interested in setting snares for rabbits. For the next week, whenever I was off duty, we walked in the woods and discussed everything around us, animals, birds, trees and flowers, about all of which he was extremely knowledgeable. He was well-read too and perhaps I showed my surprise at this rather too obviously, for there was no sign of him the day afterwards: and simple peasant though he was, I missed his company more than I cared to admit.

However, I was relieved to find him waiting for me the next day, smiling and deferential, and off we went on a highly successful pigeon shoot.

When I returned to barracks it was to learn that our Colonel had been recalled to Vienna for urgent consultations and discussion of military strategy, and as there was absolutely no sign of unrest, he had set off immediately with an escort, leaving the Captain in charge – a fair-haired man with slightly protuberant blue eyes and a splendid constitution, who thoroughly enjoyed the discipline of army life and the good food and wine of the mess.

The first evening of his command he ate and drank heartily as usual, but next morning when the orderly went to call him he found him pale, gasping for breath and talking incoherently.

'Some marsh fever,' the surgeon said, looking out of the window at the expanse of damp ground between the fence of the barracks and the river. And he gave orders for the Captain to be fed with a nourishing broth while he prepared a potion to calm him and reduce the fever.

By nightfall the Captain had rallied a little but showed no inclination to talk and refused a sleeping draught. The next day, however, the orderly was shocked to find him gasping for breath again, his cheeks pale and sunken. Again the surgeon applied his remedies, but it soon became apparent that something noxious in the night air was affecting our Captain as he grew daily weaker and more emaciated.

'If we are to save his life,' the surgeon declared, 'we must get him away from this unhealthy valley and back to Vienna. And I must accompany him on the journey, for he will need my help.'

A carriage was immediately ordered from the nearest town and a guard mounted to escort the sick Captain and the surgeon on the long journey home.

Now the Lieutenant was in charge.

He was a fine jovial fellow with thick fair hair and beard and ice-blue eyes: immensely strong, he could drink everyone else under the table.

But it was not drink that laid him low that night, for he took his new command most seriously and while he ate as usual he drank sparingly.

Early the next morning a frightened orderly wakened me and asked me to go to the Lieutenant who, it appeared, had been taken ill during the night. When I reached his room it was to find him tossing on his bed, gasping for breath, his face pale and drawn – his condition exactly as had been that of our Captain.

My position was not an enviable one. As long as he was ill, I was in charge, but I had no surgeon to advise me and help me in his treatment.

The window was open but there was not a breath of wind and the atmosphere was strangely oppressive. I gave orders for a cool draught to be brought, bent over my sick Lieutenant and tried to reassure him, and it was then that I noticed the marks on his throat. At first I took them to be freckles, but on closer examination I saw they were small wounds on which the blood had dried.

'Had the Captain such marks on his throat?' I asked the orderly.

The man looked frightened.

'Yes, Herr Cornet.'

Remembering the pretty moths of the previous night I wondered if any of them could have injected any irritant or poison while the Lieutenant slept and so I gave orders for his window to be shut that night and for a corporal to remain by his bedside and to summon me at once if the patient grew worse.

I recall wakening once during the night in a cold sweat and listening, but all was quiet and I must have fallen asleep again immediately for the next thing I knew was the duty guard shaking me and babbling with fear, begging me to come quickly.

The Lieutenant lay on his bed, pale and scarcely breathing, the marks on his throat larger and definitely red: on the floor beside an overturned chair lay the Corporal, his fair hair matted with sweat, his face devoid of all colour: his tunic and shirt were undone and his throat was marked with wounds from which blood still oozed.

Bitterly did I reproach myself for not having sat by my superior officer and faced whatever evil thing it was that had entered the barracks and attacked three of our number. Should I sent a message to my Colonel in Vienna or seek help from a doctor in the nearest town?

I cannot explain why I suddenly thought and acted as I did. But I gave orders for the two sick men to be cared for and guarded and my black stallion, Dragon, to be brought round. I galloped up the hill track to the cottage Stefan had once indicated as his home, but to which I had never gone or indeed been invited to visit.

As I reined my horse by the front door an old man came out.

'Stefan?' I asked hopefully, suddenly realizing I knew him by no other name.

The old man shook his head and spoke quickly and at some length, and as he did so I thought how foolish I had been in not attempting to learn at least a few words of the local language. Finally, by observing his gestures and the way he counted on his fingers, I gathered that Stefan was not at home but that the old man would find him and I could expect him at the barracks at noon.

It was a few minutes after twelve when Stefan was shown into the room where I sat with the two sick men, bathing their foreheads and trying to make sense of their incoherent outbreaks. I watched as he examined first the Lieutenant and then the Corporal, lifting their eyelids to gaze into their glazed blue eyes, checking their heartbeats and closely examining their throats.

'Two nights and one night, Herr Cornet?' he asked suddenly.

'Yes.'

'Are they the only ones?'

I told him about the Captain.

'On which night was he attacked?'

'Attacked? Do you mean this is the work of some enemy?' The question was out before it had occurred to me that our enemy might well be his compatriot and friend.

'Which night, Herr Cornet?' He looked older when

he frowned, and it seemed as though he had been expecting my reply for he muttered, 'Of course. When the moon was full.' He paused. 'We have met and talked several times since then. You would have done well to mention the Captain's condition to me before now.' There was both pity and scorn in those dark eyes. 'Assuredly your masters in Vienna did you no service when they sent you here to Transylvania. The Captain, I presume, was fair of hair and his eyes were blue, as are both these men?'

'Yes.'

I shuddered.

Now I remembered the old tales my nurse used to tell me when I was a boy and I recalled the delicious fear that possessed me as I heard of creatures which returned from the grave to renew their lives by drinking the blood of those still alive.

'You are telling me it is a vampire that has attacked us, Stefan?'

'No, Herr Cornet. It is you who have just told me so. But you are right.'

'And everyone nearby knows of this creature?'

'Yes.'

'Then why has no one done anything about so terrible a thing?' I demanded angrily.

'There was no need. Our vampire was content to slumber in a narrow grave until you Hussars came here, unwanted and uninvited. It was only the aristocratic blood of fair-haired, blue-eyed young men that awakened it.'

Horror chilled me, for suddenly I knew that I could be the next victim, and then, conscious of Stefan's scrutiny, I shook off my fear and stood up as straight and tall as I had been trained.

'If we have awakened this vampire by our presence, will it return to its grave if we leave Transylvania?'

'No. You Hussars have sown the wind: if you leave tomorrow – and I do not think your superiors in Vienna would allow that, for which of them would believe your tale of a vampire? – but if you leave tomorrow, then it is we who must reap the whirlwind.'

'Help me, Stefan,' I begged, throwing aside both fear and pride. 'There must be something I can do to put an end to this evil creature.'

'Perhaps there is. But it might cost you dear.'

'How dear?'

'A life.'

'Whose?'

'That I do not yet know. But this I can tell you, for it is so ordained – the only one who might prevail must be the youngest man here; he must be of the utmost integrity; and he must ride a black stallion without a single white hair on its coat.'

I hesitated. Stefan knew I was the youngest man in the troop, had heard me wax lyrical in praise of Dragon, my black stallion, and though I had been brought up to be honest and upright, I knew I had as many faults and failings as the next man.

'So,' Stefan said, as I continued to hesitate, 'we know you can satisfy two of the conditions: as to the third, we shall have proof of that, one way or another, before the night is out. I take it, then, that you are willing to help us?'

'I will do everything in my power,' I answered, and my voice trembled in spite of my trying to keep it steady.

'Good. Listen carefully for there is more at stake than any man here dreams of.

'First, bid your men carry out their duties as usual during the daylight, but tell them all to come indoors as soon as the sun begins to set and to remain together in the same room.

'Then give orders for the two sick men to be carried to that room and see that there is plenty of food but only spring water to drink.

'All doors must be locked and all windows closed. The windows of the room in which the men wait must be protected by garlic. Warn them that no matter what happens they must remain there during the hours of darkness. If you have not returned to them by the time the first cock crows we shall have failed, and they must make their way back as speedily as possible to Vienna, taking with them the Lieutenant and the Corporal, who will then, I fear, be dead: their bodies will have their own tale to tell the authorities, who will doubtless consider them the victims of cholera and agree the men were wise to leave such a pestilence-ridden place.'

'And I? You have not told me what I am to do.'

'An hour before dusk you will wait for me at the main gate of the barracks, wearing full regimental uniform and mounted on your black stallion. Make no attempt to greet me but follow me and do as I command.'

That, I think, was the longest and most terrible afternoon of my life. I gave commands with averted eyes so that I should not see the fear and concern on every face, afterwards I dressed and waited, knowing that I was to fight something evil beyond all imagination which might claim not only my life – and that, at eighteen, I must confess was very dear to me – but my immortal soul: and what would become of me then I dared not think.

An hour before dusk Stefan rode down out of the forest on a fine white stallion, the first time I had ever seen him mounted, and as I followed him on my splendid Dragon, I knew he too must have ridden almost every day of his life.

A few minutes later we were joined by another rider carrying a spade across his saddle, an unlit lantern tied to his belt, and in him I recognized the old man to whom I had spoken that morning.

For nearly an hour we rode up a winding track that climbed steeply through a dense forest, and then as the trees thinned out, we descended into a valley to which Stefan had not previously taken me, and we rode along the left bank of a swiftly-flowing river, passing first one and then another roofless house with gaping doors and windows, and walls blackened by smoke or partially consumed by fire.

What catastrophe had happened to this once prosperous village, I wondered, as Dragon picked his way over tumbled stones and charred wood and broken pottery.

At length we came to a high stone wall in good condition and outside a pair of wrought-iron gates Stefan signalled to me to wait while he dismounted and watched as the old man produced a massive key and turned it in the lock.

'Now is the testing time, Christian.'

I lowered my head in agreement. It was the first time he had used my name and had not called me Herr Cornet, but somehow this seemed right and proper, for his lineage, I was convinced, was older and prouder than mine.

'In the ruined village through which we have ridden there was once much evil: there were bitter feuds and murder, fighting and sudden deaths and people walked always in the shadow of fear until at last one who was the richest and most powerful – and the most evil – brought cholera here and all were destroyed, for no one would come to their aid.

'They are buried in the churchyard beyond these gates: men and women, boys and girls and even babies. All are now at rest save that one who brought the cholera and that is the vampire you seek and, I must warn you, who now seeks you.'

Taking the lantern from the old man he lit it and handed it to me.

'Ride slowly and with great care where once there were paths through the graveyard, keeping your black stallion on a loose rein. The moment he reaches a grave where he rears and refuses to move either forwards or backwards, dismount and call my name three times. Now go.'

Through the gates I rode into the silence of the long-neglected burial ground and by the jerking light of the lantern and the last rays of the setting sun I saw the headstones lurching drunkenly amongst the rank grass while foul-smelling, trailing plants strangled one another in their fight for survival. On I rode until I came to the desolate, roofless church and I tried hard to imagine the sound of singing and the voice of the priest, but it was as though some power was cutting off my thoughts from everything that was good and kind and true, and so I turned Dragon and skirted the sad building and rode slowly down the next path, and then up another and down a third, and over all it seemed to me there was the hush of a thousand people waiting . . . waiting . . .

And I was afraid.

Suddenly Dragon reared, nearly unseating me, then brought his forelegs down and, head drawn back and shivering, refused to move.

Dismounting I called Stefan's name three times and by the light of the lantern stared down at the tangled weeds which clung to a massive ornate headstone with funeral urns and garlands and headless cherubs, but such lettering as was not covered by plants or lichen was either worn or defaced and the only word I could make out appeared to be 'Count', and underneath a date some twenty years previous.

I glanced up as Stefan and the old man joined me and watched as the latter began to dig, marvelling at the strength in those old limbs as the earth was lifted and heaped to one side, and presently a coffin was exposed in the darkness below.

With a twist of his spade the old man had the lid off and as he handed it up to Stefan I shuddered and kept my eyes closed, for after twenty years I knew that all that could be left would be a few fragments of grave clothes and a disjointed skeleton.

'Look!' Stefan commanded fiercely, shaking me by the arm.

I opened my eyes.

Hand-embroidered green and white silk, the most intricate of fine lace, dark curls piled high above a smooth oval face, long dark lashes . . . Surely I had seen her before? But where?

'She is the most beautiful girl I have ever seen,' I whispered.

'Beautiful enough to die for?' Stefan asked softly.
'Many men did that when she was alive: many more
after she died, until at last a man of great holiness
overcame the evil spirit that possessed her, and for
some years she slept here until you Hussars, all
unknowing, gave her back her lust for blood, and the
means to satisfy it. Now lift her body out and place it
here on the ground.'

Tenderly I picked her up, amazed that I had not
realized at once how similar to Stefan's was this face.
Just as I lowered her onto the grass the moon came
out, and it seemed to me those long lashes fluttered
and the red lips parted as though a breath were
drawn.

'With a single blow strike off the head,' Stefan
ordered and put the spade into my hand.

'I cannot. That would be murder. She is alive and
so beautiful, so very beautiful.'

'Strike now before it is too late and the moon gives
her the power to destroy us all.' Stefan brought his
hand down urgently on my shoulder and in so doing
knocked off my plumet helmet so that it fell to the
ground and a soft wind ruffled my hair.

Spade in hand I looked down.

The long lashes flutterd again and for a fraction of
a moment I was staring into dark eyes of such
malignancy, into a face so grey and lined and trans-
formed by greed and lust for blood that it seemed a
thousand years old: the eyes widened at the sight of
my flaxen hair and then closed and the face was pale
and smooth again.

I was only eighteen: my emotions were confused
but amongst them there was, I swear, something akin
to love.

107

But I raised my spade and brought the sharp edge down with all my strength across that slender neck.

Never shall I forget the anguished, high-pitched shriek that filled the air or the fearful smell of spilt blood as I closed my eyes on the dreadful deed I had done.

'There is nothing to fear now, Christian,' Stefan said gently. 'See for yourself.'

The severed head with its dark curls, the silk dress and lace fichu – all had disappeared. On the ground lay a fragment of mouldering cloth, a skull and some bones.

'The Countess Elizabeth and my elder sister by twenty years,' Stefan said in a low voice.

'She was very lovely,' I stammered.

'And very evil. I would thank you for what you have done for me and my family if I could find the words – but I cannot.'

And I would have apologised for treating him like a peasant and a serf if I could have found the words – but I could not.

'My servant will take you back to your barracks. Perhaps one day we shall meet again.'

But as he rode away, I knew that soon I should be recalled from Stefan's Transylvania to serve my Emperor in far-off lands, and that a man who could have been a true friend to me had gone out of my life for ever.

9   A Highland Haunting

Having been out on his rounds since very early that
morning, Doctor John MacDonald was appreciating
his wife's jugged hare when Dorcas, the maid, tapped
on the door and opened it in haste.

'Wee Tammie's just come from Pattack Lodge with
a message from Dougal MacLean that his wife is
needing ye badly, Doctor.'

As the doctor made to rise from the table, his wife
put her hand gently on his shoulder.

'The bairn wasn't expected until March. Finish
your dinner, John, for you've a long hard ride ahead
and dear knows when you'll get another bite to eat.'
She turned to the maid. 'Tell Murdo to saddle the
mare as usual, Dorcas, and do you put up bread and
cheese and don't forget to fill the doctor's flask.'

Ten minutes later the doctor rode out of Dalwhin-
nie, leaving the main Inverness to Perth road to follow
the narrow track along the west bank of Loch Ericht.
The mare carried two saddle-bags: in one was oats, in
the other was what was locally known as the doctor's
'wee black bag' with all his medical equipment, his
food and a flask of good local whisky.

It was a pity he hadn't got the message earlier, he
thought, for February afternoons in the Grampians
were short enough at the best of times, but today the

mountains were in a sullen mood, the air damp, and mist already capping the high tops and, as the wind rose, twisting and twirling down the steep rocky slopes, filling the crevasses worn by the rushing burns.

There were no roads and no houses of any size in this part of the country, but such farms and bothies as there were all had their own tracks and the doctor was familiar with most of them. The MacLeans' place was out of his usual territory but though the only time he had visited it had been on a bright July morning, he was convinced he would have no difficulty in finding it again.

For nearly eight miles he followed the track along the bank of the loch, listening to the splash of the waters as the wind whipped up waves and blew the spray against the rocky shore and he turned up the collar of his riding coat as drizzle became rain and grey mist enveloped mare and rider.

Twice he dismounted and searched around before he found the track that led away westwards from the loch. Now he knew it would wind up and down until it reached a lochan fringed with reeds, and from there he would have to ride north and again west.

Presently he stopped to let the mare drink from a tumbling stream, and a little later gave her her head when she balked at a stretch of dangerous marshy ground, allowing her to find her own way round as he wondered how he had forgotten about that hazard, and deciding it had not existed during the hot summer months.

But surely the track was climbing too steeply?

And he was among trees where no wood should be.

Turning the mare he tried to retrace his path but he could sense the animal was uneasy and it was not long before he had to admit that he was hopelessly lost.

Dismounting again, he peered round in the rain and the mist: the mare neighed and nuzzled his wet cheek, turning the doctor's head slightly so that not far off he caught a glimpse of a faint flickering light.

'Thank goodness!' he cried, patting the mare and then leading her cautiously – for he could still make out no track – to that welcoming light. 'Whoever lives there will be able to tell me where I am and how to get to the MacLeans.'

But just as he reached the bothy the light went out.

They've gone to bed, he thought, but it won't take me a minute to rouse them; and he knocked on the door.

Within all was dark and silent.

He knocked again.

Still no reply.

The rain lashed down and the mist was thicker than ever: he'd ride no farther that night, he knew, and he made his way to a tumbledown byre he could see at the back of the cottage. Here he lit the lantern he always carried with him and, leading the mare inside, he unsaddled her and wiped her down. After making her fast to a post he poured out a generous helping of oats.

'You'll be all right here,' he said, holding up his lantern, but there was fear in the mare's eyes and his words brought her little comfort.

Back to the bothy he stumbled with his lantern and saddle-bag and once again he hammered on the door, shouted, and then tried the latch.

To his surprise the door creaked slowly open.

'Is anyone there?' he called out. 'It's Doctor MacDonald in need of a bit of shelter and help.'

There was no answer, no movement at all.

Holding up his lantern he took a couple of steps into the one-roomed bothy and suddenly stopped, staring around, gripped by some vague feeling of . . . of what? . . . an impression . . . an apprehension of something to be feared, something evil in the atmosphere of the place.

Dust and grime lay thick on the earthen floor, on the rough wooden table and on the two stools by the empty fireplace. In the darkness at the farthest end from the door was a box bed – a recess within the wall serving, as in many Highland bothies, as a place to sleep. Tattered curtains hung at the side that faced the room: a couple of worn horse blankets lay on the floor.

'It must be months, maybe years, since anyone lived here.' The doctor spoke aloud to cheer himself up. 'But I suppose I've known worse places and there are parts where the thatch hardly leaks at all.' And to overcome the strange depression and the other feeling to which he could not put a name, he set to work to gather up some dusty twigs and logs that lay to one side of the hearth: these he arranged in a neat conical fashion and soon had a fire going.

'Cheering if not exactly warming,' he commented, drawing the table and one of the stools as close as possible. Flicking the dust off with his handkerchief, he sneezed several times, blew his nose, and then unwrapped his bread and cheese, drank a wee dram, and felt greatly comforted.

'It's not a place I'd choose to spend the night,' he

112

told the fire, 'but doctors are like beggars and can't be choosers.'

He walked over to the dark corner and surveyed the box bed with its horse blankets and tattered hangings.

'Better than the floor, I suppose.'

Taking off his wet outer clothes – all a sober black becoming a doctor – he hung them on a nail in a rafter at the foot of the bed where they merged with the darkness. His silver watch he wound carefully and laid it and the chain on a three-legged stool beside the bedhead, outside the hangings but where he would see it first thing in the morning. His saddle-bag he placed under the bed, extinguished the lantern and placed it beside it, and then he clambered into the bed and pulled up the blankets. They were dirty, he knew, but somehow he had to keep warm.

Yawning, he refused to admit to the sense of unease that had been with him ever since he had stabled his mare. He was tired, that was all. And he closed his eyes and was just on the pleasant borders of being awake and drifting off to sleep when the silence was shattered by voices.

Men's voices. Raised in anger, and cursing and swearing in some strange foreign tongue.

Cautiously he eased himself up a little and peered through a tear in the hangings into the kitchen, lit by the dying embers of the fire he himself had kindled.

Two men, dirty and unshaven, their clothes worn and stained and curiously old-fashioned, sat on the stools on either side of the table where he had eaten his supper a few minutes ago.

But that was impossible.

These men had been playing cards for some time,

113

and drinking too, judging by the bottles on the floor. Cards and coins were scattered on the table and one card – the doctor prided himself on his excellent eyesight and could see it was the Four of Clubs – lay on the floor by the foot of the man whose back was towards the bed.

Angrily his partner shouted at him, obviously accusing him of cheating.

Vehemently the other denied it, spat, slammed the table with a huge, work-calloused hand. Suddenly he bent and grabbed a little wooden footstool as the nearest weapon.

At the same moment his partner rose. Big and burly, he leaned across the table. There was a flash of steel as he brought his scarred left arm down and drove a long thin knife into the back of the stooping man.

A terrible cry filled the room.

The stabbed man clutched at the table and threw the footstool wildly across the room where it splintered against the wall. Quite slowly he toppled forwards, dragging stool and table with him and he lay on the floor, blood trickling from his mouth, the handle of the knife protruding from his back, cards and money scattered around him. He moaned once, his arms and legs moved convulsively, and then he was still.

For a moment the living gambler contemplated his dead partner before scooping up the scattered cards and coins. Next he turned the still body over with one foot, searched the pockets for money and finally wrenched a gold ring off the dead man's finger: squatting on the floor he fitted the ring on to one of his own fingers, turning his hand this way and that, gloating as it gleamed in the flickering firelight.

That man on the floor is dead – murdered! – the doctor thought, horrified at the scene he had just witnessed, but knowing there was nothing he could do for the victim and realising his own life was in danger if he were discovered, he lay still in the bed, pulled the blankets up so that they covered him entirely, and waited in the darkness.

All was silent in the kitchen but soon he heard heavy footsteps approaching the bed.

He could hear the fellow breathing heavily as he stopped by the three-legged stool at the head of the bed. At that moment a log broke and flared up and the silver watch and chain must have gleamed momentarily, for the man grunted, picked them up, and after a slight hesitation turned and walked back to the dying fire. There he kicked the ash so that it burst into flame again and the doctor knew the murderer was gloating over his watch, just as he had over the stolen ring; but he dared not move from the concealing blankets.

Presently the door was opened and there was the sound of something being dragged across the floor. Then the door slammed shut and there was silence again – the silence of past violence and sudden murder.

Evidently the man was disposing of his victim. Would he come back again? Would he discover the mare in the shed?

Almost stifled by the filthy horse blankets the doctor lay without movement, listening, trying to make up his mind whether to attempt to escape now or to wait until he stood a better chance of getting away.

How quiet the room was, he thought, and gradually

his fear grew less and, overcome by fatigue, he fell into a fevered sleep.

Dawn was breaking when he awoke with a start, and even as he sat up he remembered the events of the previous night, the quarrelling card players and the brutal murder. Shuddering at the recollection, he peered into the kitchen, dimly lit by the morning sun streaming through a dusty window. To his relief the room was empty.

Had it been a dream? A nightmare? All a matter of his imagination?

The table and stools stood upright as he had left them. There were no cards, bottles or scattered coins on the dusty floor. There was no splintered footstool near the door.

He must have dreamed it.

Shivering, he jumped out of bed, put on his still damp outer clothing and dragged his saddle-bag and lantern from their dusty hiding-place.

What time was it, he wondered, turning to the stool by the head of the bed.

But there was no silver watch and chain there, although he distinctly remembered placing them there the previous night.

Frantically he searched the floor beside and under the bed. And the bed itself. Then he turned to the kitchen, his anxiety growing, for this was no ordinary watch but a cherished family heirloom.

Suddenly he remembered the man in his dream – the murderer – picking them up, taking them to the fire and gloating over them as he had over the stolen ring.

Sickened and confused, he flung open the door to

rid the place of its foetid atmosphere, and glanced around for one last look for his watch.

Only then did he see what was almost hidden by the leg of the stool.

A playing card.

Slowly he returned, picked it up and stared at it in disbelief and horror. The Four of Clubs. The same card, with its strangely old fashioned design, he had seen in his dream.

One corner of the card was red and stained. And when he looked closely at the floor where the card – and the murdered man – had lain he saw a mark which could have been a bloodstain.

The sooner I am out of here the better, he thought, thrusting the card in his pocket and picking up his bag and lantern. He looked outside to make sure no one lurked there, and then hurried to the byre, profoundly relieved to find his mare still there, and as he saddled her he sensed that her relief was as great as his own.

'Good lass!' he said, taking the reins to lead her out. 'You knew there was something wrong with this place, didn't you? Though I'm blessed if I can understand it. Whoa, there!' he called, as the mare shied at the door. Looking down he saw a splintered wooden footstool, uncannily like the one the gambler in the bothy had thrown before the knife had descended, but whether or not it had lain there in the byre the previous evening he had no idea.

'It's all right, lass,' he said, patting the mare reassuringly as he gentled her outside. Swinging himself into the saddle he rode carefully downhill until at last he recognized the track he had missed in the rain and mist, and along it he galloped.

'Doctor, I am glad to see ye,' Dougal MacLean cried, having espied the horse and rider coming up the long track to his cottage. 'The wife's awful bad and its her first, ye ken. I tellt her it was the rain and the mist holding ye up and she never compained once, poor lassie.'

Two hours later Ailie MacLean was looking down at the tiny wrinkled face of her son and smiling in wonderment.

'You didn't need me, Ailie,' Doctor MacDonald said, well-pleased that he had arrived when he did for Ailie had indeed needed his professional skill. 'After all the lambs your man's helped into the world, he'd have managed fine.'

'A bairn's no' a lamb,' Dougal said firmly. 'Ye'll have a dram now and a wee bite to eat before ye go back?'

As Ailie and the bairn slept, the two men had a meal of cold mutton and brandy and at last the doctor told Dougal of the murder he had either witnessed or dreamed about and the terrible fear that had gripped him and still lingered, even here in the peace of the shepherd's cottage.

When he finished Dougal looked at him strangely and asked him to describe the place he had left that morning.

As the doctor came to an end, Dougal drew a deep breath.

'If I'd known ye were there last nicht, I'd have come for ye myself, and not all the storms of the Grampians'd have stopped me, Doctor. Yon's a haunted bothy. Aye. Haunted! And what ye've just tellt me ye saw happened a hundred year ago – that's a fact. Exactly a hundred year ago, in 1793. My grandfather told me a tale he got from his grandfather – ye know our family's lived here for generations? Weel, two German soldiers from the army that occupied our land for years after the Forty-Five, came to yon bothy to drink and gamble away their pay. They say one of them was left-handed'

The doctor nodded slowly, remembering the flash of steel in the murderer's left hand.

'They quarrelled,' Dougal continued. 'One killed the other and vanished. The other, the murdered man, was found in a burn nearby with a knife in his back.'

There was a long silence.

'A hundred years ago,' the doctor repeated at length. 'That's odd. Very odd. 1793 is exactly the date that was inscribed on my watch. It was passed down in my family and my father gave it to me on my twenty-first birthday. Could that be just a coincidence? Or is there something more behind it all that I can't rightly understand?'

From his pocket he drew the playing card he had picked up from the bothy floor.

Dougal stared at it.

'The Four of Clubs. That's the Devil's card. They say the man that holds that never wins.' He stared even harder at the ominous stain in the corner. 'Doctor, there's only one place for that unchauncy thing.' And seizing the card he threw it into the fire, and as it curled and blackened he muttered, 'It was evil, Doctor, and noo it's returned to the flames it came from.'

Dr MacDonald was sorry that this evidence of last

night's experience had been destroyed but he agreed with Dougal. It was better that way.

As he made ready to go, he turned to the shepherd.

'Dougal, I wouldn't want anyone else to go through what I did last night. Could you pull down that haunted bothy some time? And promise me you'll tell no one else about what I've just told you.'

Dougal promised. And kept his word.

10   The Creature of Croglin Grange

The first anyone knew about it was when Henry, the head waiter at The George in Keswick, overheard the 'legal gentleman' from London asking the manager how to get to Croglin Grange and then enquiring whether there was a local builder and decorator he could recommend.

Everyone knew old Sam Graham would be offered the job. He was on the spot, living as he did less than a mile from the Grange in Croglin village: he knew his trade better than anyone in those parts: most important he was uncle by marriage to the manager.

The question was, would he take it?

Aye, Sam admitted as soon as he entered the local pub the next evening, he'd taken the job. And he waited for the comments and the jokes.

They came all right.

'Tha mun be daft to work up at Croglin again, Sam. T'bogle'll get thee sure as I'm standing here.'

'Mind tha's away before sunset or t'bogle'll have thee and we'll find thee stark stiff next morning, eyes wide and hair on end – what's left of it, of course – '

' – and not a single drop of blood left in thy veins, Sam.'

'Any bogle what sucks Sam's blood is in for a treat.

Pure alcohol, that's what it mun be now. Pure alcohol.'

The following morning the 'legal gentleman' drove up to Croglin Grange in his carriage, and there Sam met him.

'Magnificient view,' the 'legal gentleman' said, standing on the balustraded terrace in front of the long, single-storeyed stone house, and he looked down over the neglected garden to the spire of the village church rising above the trees and the lake that shimmered in the sunshine.

'Aye,' Sam agreed, but it wasn't the view he was looking at: it was the condition of the stonework and the wood of the windows and shutters.

He followed the 'legal gentleman' inside and went from room to room, checking the general structure and the furniture too, mostly just looking, sometimes pressing with his finger, frequently sniffing.

'Of course it's been unoccupied for a long time,' the 'legal gentleman' said.

'Aye. It's twenty-one years since t'Musgraves left.'

'As long as that? But our agents in the north – in York actually – had the place aired and cleaned regularly.'

'Aye. Mary Bowes and her sister what worked for t'Musgraves when they lived here. Then Mary Ann Gibson and her aunt what married a Jackson. Now it's Sarah and Eliza Richardson.'

The 'legal gentleman' was surprised that Sam knew so much. But then he didn't know the first thing about Cumbrians. And of course he didn't know that the village women always worked together in the same room, or that they were always off long before the sun set.

Because, as everyone said, it was better to be safe than sorry.

'We seem to have lost the gardener,' the 'legal gentleman' said, looking out of the window at the neglected lawns and trees and shrubs.

'He died.'

'Er – quite. I – er – don't suppose you can find another one?'

Sam gave the matter his consideration although of course he'd expected the question and had his suggestion ready.

'Joe Clifford knows a fair bit about gardens and he's a good worker. Reliable too. Need a lad to help him of course. Tha could have a word with Joe before tha drives back to Keswick.'

Joe had recently married Sam's great-niece, Isabel. And Sam knew the young couple would be glad of the cottage that went with the job.

'You are remarkably helpful Mr – er – Graham. If you could let me have your estimate some time . . .'

'Aye, that I will,' Sam said. 'It won't be any of t' family coming back?' he asked casually.

'Oh, no. They're settled in Canada. No, the Grange has been let on a long lease to three young people. Two young men and their sister. Charming. The young lady is particularly excited about coming to live here. Could it be ready for them in August, do you think?'

'Aye. If I have to take on extra men I'll let thee know. What about staff?' Sam had a number of eminently suitable relatives in mind.

'I rather think the young people mean to bring their own London staff with them.'

And that was a mistake, Sam thought, though of course he didn't say anything.

'T'Grange and t'gardens'll be ready for August first,' he promised. And so they were.

The County families of Keswick and its environs waited, wondering what the new tenants would be like and whether they were such as would be welcome to their society.

The villagers waited too. For they knew what had happened twenty-one years ago when the Musgraves had left the Grange for ever. And they knew what had happened twenty-one years before that. Or if they didn't exactly know, they had a very shrewd idea.

The new tenants of Croglin Grange were delighted with their beautiful home, and as they were pleasant and friendly – and very rich – they were immediately welcomed into Cumbrian social life. Parties were given for them, picnics organized, and they went walking in the hills and sailing on the lake. No one cared to mention the strange history of the Grange.

Both the brothers were extremely handsome and vigorous young men, but the young lady was pale and wan: perhaps the fresh mountain air and the bright sunshine would soon restore her completely to health.

She told everyone how all her life she had longed to live in just such a house that looked down on just such a village and lake.

'I even dreamed about it,' she said with a laugh. 'Imagine – I had never seen or heard of Croglin Grange but I dreamed about it many times. It seemed to call to me. I told my brothers I should not be happy until they found me my dream house. And they did. And now I am indeed the happiest person in the world.'

The three young people had lived very happily at the Grange for nearly a year when on Sunday in June they decided not to go to the church in Keswick as was their wont, but to attend the evening service in the village church.

If they'd mentioned this to Sam, he would have advised them against it. He wouldn't have mentioned the true reason of course.

So they found out for themselves that the church – however attractive it looked from their home – was cold and damp and they couldn't make out a word the parson said, because he needed new false teeth and hissed and muttered.

But the young lady smiled and her brothers bowed to everyone as they left the church and started to walk up the path through the churchyard, and then, to everyone's concern, just as she reached a vault so overgrown with moss and lichen that the names of the dead occupants could scarcely be distinguished, the young lady stumbled. Reaching out a white glove hand she grasped a cornerstone and managed to retain her balance.

'No, I'm not hurt,' she assured her brothers. 'The path is uneven.' And she tried to wipe the moss from the palm of her glove but soon gave up, knowing it would have to be washed.

No one thought to tell Sam about that either.

The following day was the young lady's twenty-first birthday, but as so many of their new friends were away on holiday, the three young people decided to postpone the celebration until the autumn, when they proposed to hold a grand ball in Keswick.

It was one of those rare, very hot days that are generally so welcome in the Lake District and the young people arranged to take their meals out on the terrace and to spend the hours reading and occasionally looking up to admire their view.

Towards evening the heat seemed to increase rather than diminish, perhaps because there was no longer even a breath of wind. Fascinated, they watched the sky darkening and the full moon begin its climb over the hills beyond the still waters of the lake. Soon the whole valley seemed to be bathed in an unearthly light: trees and shrubs threw weird shadows across the lawn and bats swooped and wheeled from their hiding-places in the barns.

For some reason the horses were restless and twice Joe – who had made himself useful as groom and general handyman as well as gardener – had to come up from his cottage to quieten them. The trouble with Joe was that though he'd married Sam's great-niece, he was a foreigner from Kendal and didn't know much about the place.

'Rats, probably,' he explained to the elder brother. 'I'll have t'dogs at 'em tomorrow.'

But the dogs were disturbed too.

'It's t'full moon,' Joe said. 'Takes 'em that way sometimes. They'e all right now though. Well, I'd best be getting back. Wife's down at t'village with her folk and I promised I'd walked her home.'

'It's Midsummer Eve,' the young lady said, as Joe walked off. 'Isn't it romantic!'

'It's also eleven o'clock,' her elder brother said,

yawning. 'I'm for bed. I haven't done anything all day and yet I feel as tired as though I'd climbed all the mountains we can see around us.'

The doors were locked and the windows closed but the shutters were left open and everyone went off to their rooms.

It is too hot to sleep and this scene is too lovely to miss, the young lady thought, and she sat up in bed and looked out of the window at all that peaceful beauty.

It was just as she decided that perhaps she was a little tired after all that she saw two red lights moving jerkily among the trees that marked the boundary of Croglin Grange.

Two people with lanterns, she thought. But are they in the churchyard or in our garden? And whoever they are, what are they doing at this time of night?

No, not lanterns.

And not two people.

She stared at the distant figures, puzzled and slightly apprehensive. Two red lights in a dark, indefinable form approached across the lawn, lost at times in the long, eerie shadows, to emerge larger, brighter and more sinister . . .

Shuddering she watched as a tall shadowy creature advanced with long loping strides towards the house, fiery red eyes fixed on the window of her room.

She tried to scream, but no sound came from her lips. If only she could jump out of bed and run to her brothers' rooms . . . but her muscles refused to obey her.

Slowly the terrible creature climbed over the balustrade and crossed the terrace where only a few hours earlier they had supped and laughed and admired the view. Horrified she stared as a hideous, shrivelled parchment face with great burning eyes pressed itself up against her window and the mouth fell open to reveal long pointed teeth.

The window is locked, she thought, shrinking back against her pillow. Nothing can get in. I am safe.

Brown skeleton fingers tapped on the window, scratching up and down, up and down, quicker and still quicker and the eyes flashed with anger and frustration.

Now the scratching stopped and there was a new sound as those horrible fingers began pecking away, faster and ever faster, loosening tiny particles from the lead until one small pane yielded and fell on to the floor.

Transfixed with terror she watched the skeleton fingers reach inside, claw about until they found the latch that closed the window, and turned it.

Throwing up the bottom half of the window the creature climbed into the room and, red eyes blazing with triumphant evil, it crossed to the bed, seized the young lady by her long hair and forced back her head, but as it sank its foul pointed teeth into her throat the pain released her from the fear which had paralysed her, and she screamed again and again and again.

There were answering shouts from the bedrooms on the opposite side of the passage, doors opened and bare feet raced along the wooden floorboards.

'What is it?'

'What has happened?'

As the younger brother flung open the door he saw his sister lying apparently lifeless across her bed, beads of blood staining her throat. The elder brother, following close behind, caught a glimpse of a shadowy creature disappearing through the window and making off down the garden with long loping strides, faster – so it appeared to him – than any normal man could run. Waiting just long enough to assure himself that his sister was recovering consciousness, he jumped from the window to follow her attacker, but there was no sign to be seen anywhere among the shrubs or the trees at the edge of the estate, and on the far side of the wall there the churchyard lay still and silent.

Deeply disturbed, he returned at length to the Grange and together the two brothers saw to their sister's injuries and comforted her, and then, in spite of the lateness of the hour, the elder brother rode off to ask for help from their neighbour, a doctor who had but recently retired from a town practice.

The doctor bathed and dressed the yound lady's wounds, talked gently to her, gave her a sleeping draught and once he was assured she would rest peacefully, rejoined her brothers.

'She remembers nothing except that she was attacked. It may have been an animal that has escaped from a travelling circus or some poor demented creature who has evaded those in charge of him.

'If you care, I could make discreet enquiries – in case there should be another attack on someone else.

'I strongly advise, however, that as soon as your sister is recovered from the shock, you leave here – travel abroad – and give her several months to forget about her dreadful experience.'

The next morning the young lady was much recovered and agreed with the doctor that it was probably a madman who had attacked her: she begged him and her brothers not to tell any of their friends: she would stay in bed for a few days on the pretence of a summer cold, she decided, and then . . .

'Then we shall go to Switzerland and France and Italy or wherever you would like to go,' her elder brother promised.

A week later their trunks were packed and they were off in high spirits to London to arrange to travel and live abroad, to make new friends in new countries.

When Sam learned that the three young people had left the Grange, he asked Isabel about it, and suddenly she remembered the trouble her Joe had had with the horses and the dogs the night she'd been down in the village with her fold.

'Full moon?' Sam asked sharply.

'Aye. That's what Joe blamed.'

'Midsummer Eve?'

'Aye.'

Sam turned and stared across the churchyard as though he was looking back a hundred years or more.

'Anything . . . well . . . happen?' he asked at length.

'Not that we ever heard. Too good for us, that London staff. Never came to our cottage or talked to Joe if they could help it.' She paused. 'About yon cleaning and dusting – '

'Aye?'

'I'm not working there alone, even in the daytime.'

'Too much work for one,' Sam said diplomatically. 'Ask thy sister to go with thee, lass. I'll arrange it wi' t' "legal gentleman".'

After that he had a word with the coachman who had driven the young people to the station and he was very relieved when he was told that all three had been laughing and joking.

130

But he couldn't help wondering.

In the end he went to the churchyard and inspected the Musgrave family vault that had been constructed over two centuries previously. It was to the right of the path that led from the lychgate to the church door. He tore away the brambles and bindweed and saw the walls were still solid, the stout oak door locked and the padlock secured with a thick iron chain.

When he asked the parson about the last burial there, the old man shook his head and said he couldn't remember.

'Forty-two years ago,' Sam prompted. 'It mun be in t'parish register.'

Together they found the register in the chest in the vestry and the parson's spectacles in his pocket, and they turned back the pages until they came to it: *Charles Edward Elliott Edmund Musgrave, died Midsummer Eve, 184–, buried Midsummer Day.*

'What happened to t'key to t'vault door and t'key to t'big iron padlock?' Sam asked.

'It was before my time,' the parson answered. 'When I came here my predecessor said the vault was closed and would never be used again.'

I bet the family threw them in the lake, Sam thought, as he thanked the old man and helped him replace the parish register in the vestry chest.

The three young people had lived abroad most happily for nearly a year when, quite suddenly, the young lady said, 'Oh, how I long to be back in the Grange again, looking down over our garden to the church and the village and that lovely lake that sparkles in the sun.'

The brothers did not think it would be wise to

return, but they had to admit their sister had quite recovered from her shocking experience, and they knew that once she set her heart on something she got her own way in the end.

And so the elder brother wrote to their solicitor in London asking him to send up their former staff and have Croglin Grange ready for them at the beginning of July. It turned out, however, that the servants had found new positions, and so once again the solicitor asked Sam for help.

July, Sam thought, much relieved, for that meant he had a year in which to make up his mind what to say about that other matter. As to domestic help, no one would sleep in, but several of his relations would go up daily from the village, with Isabel. It was only a couple of minutes walk from her cottage to the Grange.

He'd just made all the necessary arrangements for the Grange when he got a very good offer of a job at Workington, so off he went, thinking all the time that other matter had something to do with Midsummer Eve.

No one thought to let him know when the young people arrived unexpectedly at Croglin Grange on the eighth of June.

Only Isabel wondered.

The trouble was she didn't know for sure.

And she too thought that if anything did happen, it would be at the same time as last year – Midsummer Eve.

She didn't know that it was the full moon that did it.

And that was eleven days earlier than last year.

And the day after the young people returned.

It wasn't even as though she could look up and see the moon for herself, for the sky had been black and heavy with storm clouds for nearly a week.

In the end she wrote a hurried note to her great-uncle, caught the evening collection and knew he'd get it at Workington the next day.

'How I love the rain of Cumberland!' the young lady cried, as she stepped out of her carriage and ran up the steps to the balustraded terrace, and she would have stood there until her clothes were soaked had not her brothers urged her, laughing, indoors.

It rained all afternoon and all evening but she was so happy to be back at the Grange that of course her brothers were well content. Nevertheless that night they locked all the outside shutters, checked that the windows were closed and the doors secured, and each young man loaded his pistol and put it on the table beside his bed where it would be but the work of a moment to seize it.

'How did you sleep?' they asked their sister the next morning, for they in their anxiety had tossed and turned and had not dared to close their eyes.

'Well indeed, dear brothers,' she answered happily. 'My sleep was quite untroubled, and – ' she looked out as the wind drove the rain in sheets against the window so that it ran like a waterfall down to the terrace – 'I still love the rain of Cumberland.'

It rained all that day in Workington too and Sam and his men were wet to the skin and glad when the time came to return to their lodgings. There was a letter in Isabel's handwriting waiting for Sam but he was in such a hurry to change and eat that he had no time to open it.

He'd just have a couple of pints and then an early

night, he decided. But the company was good and so was the beer, and when he came out of the little inn it had stopped raining and there up in the sky was a great round white full moon. His hand closed on the letter he'd got from Isabel and he stopped under a gas lamp and read it.

Immediately his feeling of well-being vanished, and he was off to the stables to hire a horse to get him back to the Grange even though it might now be too late.

That night the two brothers slept soundly: as they had stayed awake the previous night who could blame them? And they knew the doors were locked and bolted, the windows closed and shuttered.

The young lady slept too.

Uneasily.

Dreaming.

The dream turned into a nightmare.

Razor-sharp claws were tearing at the wooden shutters until the bolts yielded.

Gasping, she work with a start and sat up in bed to see the hideous parchment face pressing itself against her window, the terrible red eyes fixed on her, gloating in evil anticipation.

There was no slow scratching and picking this time.

The window crashed open and the creature was upon her, but the noise of the breaking glass and her terrified scream had alerted her sleeping brothers.

Even as the withered claw clutched at her hair and the malevolent face bent over her throat, the bedroom door was flung open.

Rage and frustration replaced the gloating look in the dreadful eyes as the intruder ran to the window and cleared the sill and the jagged broken glass in a bound. Swiftly the younger brother fired his pistol, but the creature swerved and jumped from the balustrade on to the lawn.

Carefully the elder brother took aim. And fired.

For a moment it seemed that the moving figure strumbled and almost fell, and then it continued with long loping strides and it seemed to the brother that it climbed over the churchyard wall and disappeared among the shadows.

'One of us must follow and capture him,' the younger brother cried.

'A ghost!' the young lady whispered, terrified, pointing to a white figure running across the lawn.

'Don't shoot,' a voice called out. 'It's only me, Isabel. Open the door for pity's sake, and let me in.'

At once the brothers unlocked the door and the housekeeper in her white nightgown ran in and flung her arms round the young lady and comforted her softly. And then she advised the brothers not to go in pursuit that night.

'There is nothing you can do and I'm quite sure there is no more danger here this evening. Help is on the way, for my great-uncle Sam'll be back soon. He'll tell you what must be done for he knows the secret of this terrible affair.'

She slept in the young lady's room and the brothers stayed on guard, one by the window and the other by the door, but there was no further disturbance.

The next morning a lad from the village brought a message to the young people: Sam had returned from Workington and would they meet him at the lychgate at the church at midday? Isabel said she would go too to look after her young mistress.

At the Lychgate, Sam gave a quick nod of acknowledgement, picked up his lantern and builders' tools, and led the way up the path to the Musgrave family vault, and the others watched as he cut through the thick iron link that held the padlock, and then seized an axe and smashed open the locked door. Lighting his lantern he held it so that the others could see the stone steps leading down into the darkness under the earth.

On both sides of the vault were shelves on which were the elaborately-decorated coffins of long-dead Musgraves.

At the far end lay one plain wooden coffin, the lid slightly to one side, and now Sam held the lantern close so that all could see the simple inscription on it: *Charles Edward Elliot Edmund Musgrave*, and underneath the date of his birth. And that of his death.

'There must have been some mistake,' the elder brother said, bewildered. 'That would mean he was a hundred and fifty years old when he died.'

Without speaking Sam lifted off the lid and there, on a torn and crumpled shroud the creature lay. He might have been made of parchment, so brown and shrivelled was his skin as it clung to his bones: at the end of the claw-like hands were curved nails, and now they could all see the long pointed teeth in the sagging jaw: in the right knee a bullet-wound had smashed the patella to fragments.

The sunken eyes appeared dull and lifeless – except that for one moment it seemed to Sam he caught a flicker of movement there.

'Folks always said he were a wild one. Made t'country too hot for him and when he were twenty he took off for strange places – Hungary and Russia and China. That were nigh on two hundred year ago.

136

'My grandpa were a lad and working up t'Grange when he returned forty-two years ago. Young he seemed and boasted he had t'secret of eternal life from some heathen in Canton in China. Said he'd come back to join t'family. Had his eyes on Miss Julia all that evening. And him a hundred and fifty but looking as young and handsome as his protrait that used to hang in t'library. But evil, so my grandpa said. Aye. Evil.

'But t'very next morning after he came back he was found lying on t'lawn at t'foot of t'steps – dead. Seemed as though his old body had given out at last after all them years. They say he looked his real age too – aye, he'd been on earth a right long time, had Charles Musgrave.

'And Miss Julia were dead too. Dead in her bed and not a drop of blood left in her body. Folks blamed Charles Musgrave and his Chinese secret for that. So they buried him here, but Miss Julia they buried in Keswick. 'Twere best that way.

'There were no more trouble until twenty-two year ago when Miss Mary came of age. They gave a dinner party for her and I were helping out in t'kitchen. Next morning Miss Mary were dead in her bed and not a drop of blood left in her body.

'They buried her in Keswick too, padlocked this vault, shut up t'Grange and went off to live in Canada. They were safe with t'sea between them, and they thought it were only Musgraves that Charles Musgrave wanted.

'So did I.

'All of us in t'village knew he got out at times and scared folks: but he never attacked no one. Can't understand why thee . . .' he looked at the young lady.

137

'Did you say Charles Musgrave came back from Canton forty-three years ago?' the elder brother asked.

'Aye.'

'Our mother was born there and in that very year. Our sister was born there too, twenty-two years ago on Midsummer Eve.'

'He knew! He knew!' The young lady shivered and Isabel put a protective arm round her. 'It was he that called me – not the house. He wanted me just as he wanted the others.'

'He reckoned without thy brothers,' Sam said grimly, and this time as he looked down he saw there was indeed a flicker of movement in those dull sunken eyes and he knew Charles Musgrave for the vampire he was.

And so did all the others.

They carried the coffin out of the vault and bore it to the corner of the churchyard. There Sam lifted out the shrivelled corpse in its tattered shroud and placed it on the ground and then, with one powerful thrust, he drove a stake through its heart. A terrible unearthly shriek escaped from those dry lips and even as they watched, horrified and shuddering, the parchment body shrank and disintegrated to the finest dust and even that disappeared among the lush June grass.

And they all knew then that at last the evil spirit had been laid in that quiet churchyard by the sparkling waters of the lake, and never again would it seek its prey in Croglin or elsewhere.